Witch Silver

Anne Forbes

Witch Silver

 Kelpies

Kelpies is an imprint of Floris Books

First published in 2010 by Floris Books

The publisher acknowledges a Lottery grant
from the Scottish Arts Council towards the
publication of this series.

British Library CIP Data available
ISBN 978-086315-744-8
Printed in Poland

For my New Zealand cousin, Yvonne Stanfield

Contents

1. Lady Merial

The witch opened the door of the old, rambling, grey-stone house and closing it slowly behind her, caught a last glimpse of the familiar black and white tiles that chequered the hall floor. She sighed and a flicker of sadness crossed her face. Saying goodbye was never easy ... even for witches. Not, mind you, that she looked anything like a witch. Indeed, had you been there, watching, you'd probably have found her a bit of a disappointment for, as witches go, there was really nothing at all remarkable about her — not so much as a trace of flowing black robes, far less the usual pointed hat and certainly nothing that looked even remotely like a broomstick.

No, to the casual observer, she was just a little old lady in a worn dark coat; rather ordinary, really. Except for her eyes, that is. They weren't ordinary at all. They were sharp, black and fierce as they lifted to scan the far reaches of her garden.

A slight, somewhat rueful, smile curved her lips. The vicious gust of wind that swept across the lawn and the swirling mass of clouds that loomed over the trees beside the river told her that they were there already, waiting for her.

She could sense them and didn't so much as bat an eyelid as they materialized before her in a sharp crack of sound. Although she'd become accustomed to their sudden appearances, she nevertheless stiffened at the sight of them. Her hands clenched and her eyes narrowed. So many of them! They were obviously, she thought sourly, going to see her off in style.

These, by the way, were what you might call "proper" witches. Earth Witches, to be precise. You could tell that from the trailing roots and scabs of earth that clung to their shabby, black robes. Although there were a lot of old hags amongst them, most of them looked quite young; but they were fearsome creatures, nevertheless, their strong faces bold, wicked and cruel. She frowned. This, she hadn't expected. There must be hundreds of them, moving like a rippling tide over her front lawn.

It was then that the Wind Witches appeared on their broomsticks, swooping overhead like evil, grey shadows. The Queen of the Wind Witches, taking in the situation at a glance, promptly sent a gust of wind through the ranks of the Earth Witches and hid a satisfied smile as it played havoc with their cloaks and sent them grabbing frantically for their hats.

Watching from the top of the steps, the witch almost smiled. Not a lot had changed over the years, she mused; still the same old rivalries. The Wind Witches, it would seem, were obviously determined not to be left out of the drama that was about to unfold and she'd bet a pound to a penny that the pushy Snow Witches, too, would want to be "in" on the action. They weren't far off either and she smiled sourly as she caught a glimpse of them, slipping from the skirts of the thick, heavy clouds that rolled in livid shades of brown and purple over the house. Yes, they had all come ... anxious, no doubt, to see the back of her.

Her death would, she supposed, be quite an event in the world of magic and as Maritza, the Queen of the Earth Witches approached, she wondered idly who else would be watching; her father, perhaps? She couldn't tell and he'd given her no sign. It was hurtful, she thought sadly, but only to be expected. The Lords of the North, however, would certainly be watching, as would the MacArthurs, Lady Ellan and perhaps even Prince Kalman and Lord Rothlan. She smiled faintly as she thought of him for it had been Rothlan who had advised her against marrying a human: always headstrong, however, she'd brushed his arguments aside and given up her magic life without a second thought.

And really, she hadn't regretted marrying David. It was just a pity, she sighed inwardly, that humans lived for such a short time. But yes, they'd all be watching through their crystal balls for it was in their interests to see who would inherit the talisman; the shining silver clasp that held so much power. Over the years, she had been careful to use its magic well and, indeed, had found it remarkably easy to keep the witches in check. Scotland had prospered. No harvests had been ruined by plague or pestilence, no floods had ravaged the countryside and fierce storms had been kept to a minimum, despite the desperate pleas of the Wind Witches and the furious arguments of the Snow Witches. She smiled as she thought of how they'd sulked at not having their own way.

Nevertheless, she was well aware that behind the anger in their eyes lay the knowledge that she was no longer immortal. Human life was short and yes, they could afford to wait — after all, time was on their side.

And now, it would seem, the time had come ...

Well, she thought, she'd made her decision and hopefully it would prove to be the right one for, after much soul-searching, she'd decided to leave the talisman to her niece. Who else could she leave it to? Not to any of the witches, that was for sure, and certainly not to her father after the way he'd treated her. No, she thought, Clara was the only choice. She'd heard of her adventures from the MacArthur and knew her to be both brave and sensible. She wore a firestone, was involved in magic and she was sure that the MacArthur would advise her and do what he could to protect her. Still, she bit her lip, well aware of the consternation that her decision was going to cause.

Heaving a sigh, she turned her attention once more to the Earth Witches who, regaining their composure as well as their hats, now surged forward; their queen halting at the foot of the flight of steps. The Queen of the Earth Witches was decidedly prettier than the others. Her long, black hair curled gracefully and she had some sense of dress for there was no speck of sand or soil on her silken robes.

The old lady regarded her somewhat guiltily for Maritza was her cousin and as well as shielding her from her father's wrath, had immediately admitted her into the ranks of the Earth Witches when she had arrived in Scotland with David. The thought had sometimes crossed her mind that had she not possessed the talisman, she might have been a shade less welcome but the fact remained that the Queen of the Earth Witches had stood by her in her time of need.

The problem, now, she sighed, was the talisman. She knew perfectly well that over the years Maritza had grown to expect it — and, from the look of her as she stepped forward to speak, was behaving as though it were already hers.

Always inclined to the dramatic, the Queen of the Earth Witches raised her arms so that her cloak fluttered in the wind. "The time has come, Lady Merial," she said clearly, "for you to leave the human world. We will all grieve your passing." She paused as there was a murmur of assent from the witches. "It is my hope, however," she continued, rather less confidently, "that before you leave us, you will pass the magic talisman into my keeping for I, an Earth Witch, am your cousin and it is right that it should be mine!"

Her face was solemn as she spoke but her eyes gleamed with anticipation and at her words, a growling ripple of breathless excitement swept the ranks of the witches.

The talisman! It would soon be theirs!

The old lady's eyes narrowed. The words were little more than she had expected. Now came the tough part and, conscious of the dismay her decision was going to cause, she took a rather deeper breath than normal. "As you say, Maritza, the time has come for me to leave this world but, I'm afraid I must disappoint you, my dear, for I do not plan to leave the talisman in your care."

Maritza gasped audibly, totally taken aback. A terrible silence fell. It lasted for the best part of a minute and would have gone on for longer had the Queen of the Wind Witches and the Queen of the Snow Witches not swooped down to land beside Maritza, robes rustling and black eyes glistening with sudden hope.

The Queen of the Earth Witches ignored them. By this time, she was shaking with bewildered fury. "But ... you *must* give me the talisman, Merial," she hissed. "You know as well as I do that it is mine by right. *Mine!*"

There was a growl of agreement from the Earth Witches who piled forward in a surging crowd behind her.

"That's not quite true, Maritza," Wanda, Queen of the Wind Witches, pointed out with false sweetness. "There's nothing to stop Lady Merial from giving the talisman to me if she deems you ... unsuitable."

The Queen of the Snow Witches, incredibly beautiful in the shredded chiffon of her ivory robes, stiffened at these words. "Or, of course, to *me*," she interrupted quickly in her clear, cold voice; throwing a positively poisonous look at the Queen of the Wind Witches as she spoke.

Maritza's face contorted with anger and, with visions of the talisman slipping from her grasp, totally lost the plot. *"Unsuitable!"* she screamed, almost incoherent with rage. "How can you say that? I am *not* unsuitable!! *I am not!"*

Lady Merial glanced shrewdly from one witch to the other. "The truth is," she said, raising her hand commandingly, "that I can trust none of you to wield the power of the talisman with proper care. You, Samantha," she looked at the Queen of the Snow Witches sternly, "would cover Scotland in twenty feet of snow, given half a chance, and delight in so doing. And you, Wanda," she eyed the Queen of the Wind Witches sternly, "you, I know, would bring gales and storms to the land and take great pleasure in sinking ships at sea." She smiled thinly as Wanda's face turned black with fury as the truth of this assertion hit home.

She then turned to Maritza, her gaze thoughtful. "You are my cousin, Maritza, and I would not have you think me ungrateful. You have treated me as one of your own for many years now ..."

"Then give me the talisman, Merial! You know I always expected it to be mine!"

Lady Merial smiled, her eyes softening. "Maritza, Maritza, I know to my despair, exactly what you are capable of. You would blight the land, wouldn't you," she said softly. "You'd hex the corn so that the harvests would fail and the cattle would sicken and die."

"And the rivers," Maritza added, forgetting herself completely, "don't forget the rivers," she crooned. "I could poison their waters and kill all ... the ... fish ..."

There was a deadly silence as Wanda and Samantha, thin-lipped and furious, glared at the hapless Maritza, who, realizing what she had just said, clapped a hand over her mouth.

"Quite so," Lady Merial said, raising her arms for calm as a dismayed tide of sound rippled through the assembled witches. "Now you know why I could never trust any of you with the talisman."

There was an awful silence and she let it last before speaking again. "The talisman," she continued, ignoring the glint of venom that now smouldered behind their sullen glances, "was gifted to me by my father, Lord Jezail. As you know, he cast me off when I married a human and I have neither seen nor heard from him since. Nor do I expect to. As Wanda says, the talisman is mine to give where I please and although I agree that Maritza has a claim to it, I cannot give it to her or, indeed, to any of you."

"May we ask why, Lady Merial?" the Queen of the Wind Witches demanded.

"Witches are evil by nature," the old lady said, "but as you know, I am not a true witch despite being Maritza's cousin."

"Through another unsuitable marriage!" snapped the Queen of the Snow Witches.

"Quite," admitted Lady Merial, "but the fact remains that I am the daughter of a magician and it is the task of magicians to keep a balance between the nature of the earth and those who would destroy it."

"If you mean us, why don't you say so?" the Queen of the Wind Witches snapped, her silken grey robes rustling in the breeze.

"Read my words as you will," Lady Merial shrugged, "but that's why I've hidden the talisman."

"We'll find it," Wanda replied confidently. "Wherever you've hidden it; we'll find it!"

"We'll look everywhere," snarled Maritza, backing her up. *"Everywhere!"*

Samantha stood straight and tall. "What's hidden," she observed icily, "can be found!"

There was a murmur of agreement as each witch secretly determined, there and then, to be the one who found the talisman.

"In the meantime," Lady Merial said pointedly, "I have urgent business to attend to — and so, may I remind you, have you!"

They parted before her as she walked down the steps, curtseying deeply as she made her way through them to her car. Even as she reached it, however, they disappeared; fading away on a sighing whisper of wind. And as they disappeared, the livid banks of cloud above the house released the first few gentle flakes of snow; flakes that grew swiftly in number as the witches wove their spells.

The engine of the powerful car roared to life as the snow started to fall in earnest and, driven by a steadily rising wind, whipped quickly into a raging blizzard. Releasing the hand brake, the old lady leant forward slightly to take a last, long look at the old house before setting off amid the whirling snow. She knew exactly where they would hex her. There was a nasty curve in the road near the old quarry. It would be there.

Hidden among the trees at the side of the house, an old man, grey-haired and stooped with age, watched the car disappear and heard the noise of the engine change as it paused briefly at the imposing stone gates that marked the end of the driveway, before turning slowly onto the main road.

Shivering slightly in the freezing air, he waited until all was quiet before making his way through the snow to the front door, hexing it open as he approached; for he knew perfectly well that if he was going to find the talisman before the witches returned, he was going to have to be quick.

2. Lord Jezail

Far away, in a small, heavily wooded country on the fringes of Central Europe, Lady Merial's father, Lord Jezail, sat in the topmost tower of his great citadel. Hunched over a glowing crystal ball, he listened with a stony face to the threats of the witches and watched as they disappeared amid the rising storm.

Gorgeously dressed in velvet robes, he was an impressive figure despite his age. A mane of dark hair hung to his shoulders, bushy eyebrows flared above shrewd black eyes and a beak of a nose towered above lips that could smile charmingly when it suited him. This air of somewhat austere kindliness, however, hid a cruel, vindictive nature and although he was generally regarded as a wizard of integrity, he was, actually, nothing of the sort. Indeed, he had quite successfully hidden his true character from the world of magic for more years than he cared to remember.

Leaning back in his chair, he raised his eyes briefly to meet those of the other occupant of the room and together they looked on in silence as his daughter's car, half hidden by what was now a raging blizzard, moved slowly down the driveway towards the main road.

Had he held the eye of the crystal on the house for just a few seconds longer, he would have seen the shambling figure of the old man as he approached the house — and would, most certainly, have recognized him, perhaps even have hexed him. But, as it happened, he didn't. The crystal followed the car and the moment was lost.

"Well, Vassili," Lord Jezail muttered a few minutes later as the crystal dimmed and became misty, "what do you make of that, then?"

His aide, Count Vassili, dark-haired and slim in the elegant robes of his calling, inclined his head. Years of serving his master had taught him to choose his words carefully and although he'd been asked for his opinion in quite a few tight situations, nothing quite compared to the enormity of this one.

"Milord, what can I say? I ... I am terribly, terribly sorry. To lose your daughter like this ..." he gestured vaguely and his voice petered out as his master looked at him in surprise.

"Sorry?" Lord Jezail seemed puzzled. "Sorry? Oh, I see," he waved his hand irritably, "yes, well, it *is* a pity, I suppose, but then she always knew that this was going to happen to her, didn't she?" His face darkened and anger gleamed once more in his black eyes. "Serves her right for marrying a human!" he added coldly. "But that isn't what I meant!" he leant forward, frowning darkly. "I want to know what you think of her hiding the silver talisman!!" His voice rose in anger. "*Hiding it*, Vassili!" he repeated.

Vassili tried not to look shocked and it was only with a great effort that he managed to keep his face blank. He'd always known that Lord Jezail had a pretty cold heart but, until now, hadn't realized just how frozen it must be — for incredible as it seemed, it was obvious that even at a time like this, all he could think of was the talisman!

"I ... er, I can't believe it, milord," Vassili looked at him helplessly, throwing his hands out in disbelief.

Lord Jezail eyed him sourly, drawing his fur-lined cloak around him with a sweeping gesture that all but knocked the crystal off its stand.

Noting the twitching eyebrows and tight set of his master's lips, the count bowed low and eyed him watchfully as he rose angrily to his feet and started to pace the floor.

"How could she *do* this to me?" Lord Jezail muttered, his voice rising. "My own daughter," he said, "hiding the talisman not only from the eyes of the world of magic but from *me,* her own father."

Vassili made a vague noise that could have meant anything.

"She knew perfectly well what was going to happen to her!" his master added. "Why the devil didn't she send it back here?" He turned round and glowered accusingly at the count as though it were all his fault.

"I'm sure ..." Vassili attempted to soothe his master's anger but wasn't given the chance to finish his sentence.

"I should *never* have given it to her in the first place!" Lord Jezail continued. "I must have been mad to even *think* of it!"

"Forgive me for asking," Vassili ventured as his master continued to pace the room, "but what is it that's so ... well, special about the talisman?"

Lord Jezail turned and looked at him through hooded eyes. "Well, to begin with, its magic is extremely powerful and it protects its owner from danger of any sort," he explained. "That was the reason I gave it to Merial in the first place; to protect her from harm. But it has many other magical properties; it can cure evil spells and has great power over nature. That's one reason why the witches must never have it, for in the wrong hands they could, and would, use it to cause earthquakes, tidal waves and hurricanes; to say nothing of drought, flood and famine."

"But the witches have that power already," Vassili pointed out, "and so do you," he added reasonably. "Why, even I can call up storms and the like *and,*" he deftly slipped in the compliment, "I'm nowhere *near* as great a magician as you are, milord!"

"Ah, but the talisman can control the witches and the storm carriers," Jezail answered. "It works for the good of the earth. That's why Merial couldn't ..." he stopped in mid-sentence "... that was why she couldn't leave it to any of the witches."

"You said that before," Vassili acknowledged.

"Yes, but the point is that she *must* have known that in so doing she was virtually leaving the talisman to *me*." Lord Jezail replied.

Vassili eyed him warily.

"Think about it," his master smiled, rubbing his hands together almost gleefully. "She's hidden it!

It has no owner now that she's gone; which means, Vassili, that as I gave it to her as a gift, it is mine by right! It must return to *me*!"

Vassili nodded, his mind working swiftly. "Yes," he agreed, "yes, it *would* work like that, milord. But ... what if the witches find it? I mean ..."

"Let them find it," Lord Jezail said, smiling nastily. Vassili looked at him, startled. "It will save us the trouble of looking for it," he pointed out coldly, "and if we keep an eye on the witches through the crystal, we can take it from them whenever it's found!"

3. Craiglaw House

"It's strange being here without Auntie Muriel and Uncle David, isn't it?" Neil said wistfully to Clara, as they entered the hall. His father, elbowing the heavy door shut, dumped a pile of carrier bags on the black and white tiles and put his car keys on a side table. "I can remember Auntie Muriel giving me a real telling off for sliding down the banisters."

"Quite right, too," his father said. "You ought to have had more sense!"

Neil grinned unrepentantly. "Uncle David thought it was funny. He said it was a pity he was too old to join in!"

A look of sadness shaded John MacLean's eyes. He missed his only brother and was glad that over the years they'd managed to visit quite often. Edinburgh wasn't that far away and they'd driven down frequently for the odd weekend. And now the house was his. He couldn't quite believe it. Losing David had been bad enough but Muriel's death in a car crash had been totally unexpected.

Clara looked at the wooden staircase that curved gracefully up to the first floor. "I still can't believe we're going to live here, Dad," she said, her face shining happily. "I've always loved Craiglaw House. Auntie Muriel knew I did." Tears blurred her eyes suddenly. "I just can't believe she's gone ..."

Her mother appeared from the living room. "I thought I heard the car," she said, hugging them all. "How was the drive down, John?"

"Dad got stuck behind a couple of combine harvesters!" Neil grinned.

"It was fine," her husband answered, cuffing Neil playfully. "We stopped off for ten minutes at Blackriggs Farm on the way. You remember, Jimmy MacFarlane's place?"

"Mmm," Janet MacLean nodded. "How's the farm doing?"

"Not too well, I gather. He didn't have time to say much but his kids have fairly grown. The youngest has just started school."

"They're really into horses, these days," Clara said enthusiastically. "I wouldn't mind a pony. Once we've settled in, that is," she added hastily.

"Once we've settled in, we'll talk about it," her mother said, smiling at her enthusiasm. Moving from a busy, bustling city like Edinburgh to a remote country house was a big step and she hadn't quite known how the children would take it. She didn't have to look at Neil's face to know that he had reservations since it wasn't only the city he'd miss; it was the world of magic.

If the truth be told, she was secretly quite relieved that they had left Edinburgh — for the MacArthurs, the magic people who live inside Arthur's Seat, the huge hill that dominates the city, had, over the years, succeeded in dragging the family into all sorts of hair-raising adventures involving magicians, magic mirrors and flying horses to say nothing of some particularly nasty goblins. She was, in actual fact, very fond of the MacArthurs; enjoyed their company and loved Arthur, their great red dragon, but ...

"Won't you miss Edinburgh, Clara?" Neil queried doubtfully. "Not school particularly, I mean the MacArthurs and Arthur and ... and our magic carpets and all. We're really too far away from Edinburgh to call them like we used to. I mean, it'd take ages for them to arrive, for a start."

"You'll soon get used to living in the country," his father interrupted cheerfully, "and you'll still be able to visit the MacArthurs from time to time, you know."

"And you have to remember, too, that we've been very lucky, Neil," his mother added. "If your Uncle David and Aunt Muriel hadn't left the house to us, we would never have been able to afford anything as grand as this," she pointed out gently.

"I know," Neil muttered, "it's just that we don't know anybody here."

"It'll work out fine, Neil," his father smiled, "and once you start at Netherfield, you'll get to know lots of boys your own age."

"And girls," Clara added. "It'll be funny being boarders, though."

"That won't be for long," her mother assured her, with a quick look at her husband. "Dad's contract finishes at Christmas so you'll only be boarders for a term. And since your old school's marked down for closure, it's pointless, really, starting at a new school in Edinburgh for just one term, isn't it?"

"I suppose so," Clara admitted.

"Don't forget that you'll be spending Saturdays and Sundays here with us," her father smiled, ruffling her hair. "We'll be down more or less every weekend to check up on the builders, and sort out any problems."

"Why don't you both go upstairs and have a look at your rooms," their mother suggested with a twinkle in her eyes. "I forgot to tell you that the painter finished them yesterday. Oh, and I've left some carpet samples on the chest in the upstairs hall so that you can choose a colour you like," she called after them as both children raced up the stairs in sudden excitement.

"How have you been managing on your own then, Janet?" John MacLean asked as he followed his wife into the living room and looked round appreciatively at the polished woodwork, gleaming windows and cheerful chintz sofas grouped round the huge fireplace. It was a comfortable room and he could imagine relaxing in front of a roaring blaze of logs when winter came and snow blocked the roads.

His wife put her finger to her lips and, walking over to the door, shut it carefully.

John raised his eyebrows. "Why the secrecy?" he asked, half laughing.

"Can I ask you a question first?" she asked seriously.

"Of course! Fire away!"

"Are you wearing your firestone?"

"Wearing my firestone!" he repeated blankly. Of all the questions she could have asked, this was the last he'd have thought of; for firestones were the magic stones the MacArthurs had given them so that they could fly on magic carpets and merge with people, birds and animals.

"Are you?" she insisted.

"Well, no," he replied. "I'm not. You know perfectly well that I don't wear it all the time. Neither do you, for that matter."

"I know," she said, wringing her hands. "I wish I'd thought of it before. I'd have asked you to bring mine down with you today."

"Whatever for?" Her husband looked baffled. "There's no magic here ... is there?"

"Well, there might be. I hate to say it, John," she said hesitantly, for she knew how much he loved the house, "but there's something really strange going on."

"Strange?" he frowned questioningly. "What, here? In the house?"

Janet nodded. "I think it's haunted," she said firmly. "I'm not imagining it," she added quickly as he opened his mouth to scoff at the notion. "There are definitely ghosts around. They're not in the room at the moment," she added. "I can tell when they're nearby. There's a ... sort of a different feel to the atmosphere whenever they come in."

"Ghosts?" her husband repeated. "Are you sure? I mean, David and Muriel never said anything about the house being haunted."

"Quite sure. It's weird, really. They ... they seem to realize that I can feel them in the room and when I come in they ... well, they slip away and go somewhere else. I get the impression that they're looking for something."

"How very odd," he frowned, putting an arm round her. "Bear up, Janet. We'll sort it out, don't worry. Now, tell me all about it."

"It started when you left last week with the children. I thought I was imagining things at first and ... what on earth was that?" She froze as a scream rang through the house.

"That's Clara's voice!" John MacLean was out of the room and halfway up the stairs when Clara ran onto the landing. "Stop her, Dad!" she yelled. "Stop her!"

"Stop who?" her father asked, genuinely puzzled.

"There! Can't you see her?"

"I can't see anyone apart from the pair of you," her father answered, reaching the landing and turning to peer down the stairs. "What's going on? Who did you see?"

"Chill, Clara! She's gone now," Neil said, his eyes alight with excitement. "Straight through the front door like a bat out of hell!"

As the front door, a massive piece of solid oak, was firmly shut, his father raised his eyebrows. "What went through the door like a bat out of hell?"

"You'll never believe it, Dad," Clara said, shivering suddenly as she gripped the banister tightly, "but it was a witch! A horrible, nasty, evil-looking witch!"

4. Witch watch

"A witch?" her mother said, hugging her hard. "Here, in the house?" Meeting her husband's eyes in sudden understanding, she looked thoughtful. "I wonder if *that's* what's been going on!"

Neil's head jerked. "If *what's* been going on, Mum?" he queried.

"Come down to the kitchen and I'll tell you while I get dinner ready," his mother said, looking searchingly at Clara. "It's given you a shock, hasn't it?"

"It has a bit," Clara admitted. "She was awful-looking."

"Was she a Snow Witch?" Neil asked as they went into the kitchen and slid along the bench seat that ran along one side of the table.

Clara shook her head, remembering the Snow Witches that had captured her in Argyle. "The Snow Witches were beautiful," she said, "but this one was a proper witch, dressed in black with a sort of squidgy pointed hat and a hooked nose."

"Tell us what happened, Clara," her dad said quietly, drawing a chair up, "from the very beginning. You ran upstairs with Neil ... now go on from there."

"Well, we both went into our own rooms," Clara began. "Mine's lovely, by the way. I really like it ..."

"And ..." her father said encouragingly.

"I heard Neil opening cupboards and stuff so I thought I'd grab the carpet samples first. I sat on my bed and was turning them over, one by one, on the ring thing when ... when this witch walked into my room. Cool as you please as though she owned the place! I gave a bit of a jerk and the samples fell off the bed and while I faffed around picking them up, I decided to pretend I couldn't see her. I sat on my bed again, got the samples organized and kept turning them over, matching them up to the duvet cover. And all the time, the witch sat in the chair by the window watching me. That's all she did. Sat and stared. She didn't have a clue that I could see her."

"What happened next?" her mother asked anxiously.

"Well, I thought she might get fed up and leave so I looked up and gazed straight at her. And then she suddenly realized that *I* was watching *her*. Honestly, it was almost funny! She sort of sat up and stared. She knew by my eyes that I could see her." Clara almost smiled. "Her mouth dropped open and she looked ..."

"Totally gobsmacked!" grinned Neil.

"Yes, I suppose so. And then she went all fierce and evil and I thought she was going to hex me. That's when I screamed and she buzzed off."

Janet MacLean looked worriedly at her husband but Neil and Clara eyed one another excitedly.

Witches! Life in the country was certainly looking up!

Just then the telephone rang. John picked up the receiver. "Hello," he said. "Hello? Oh, it's you, Jimmy. Hi."

As he talked, Mrs MacLean turned to Neil and Clara and in a low voice, told them what had been happening in the house while they had been in Edinburgh.

"So now you think your ghosts might be witches?" Neil asked doubtfully.

"It seems more than likely," his mother reasoned. "After all, Clara said that the witch walked into her bedroom as though she owned the place." She shook her head worriedly. "It looks as though the house has been more or less a den of witches ever since Muriel died! They feel at home here, for goodness sake!"

Clara nodded, looking around the room, feeling excited and scared at the same time.

"There aren't any witches in the room just now," her mother said grimly. "I know the feel of them when they're around only too well. They've been keeping me company all week!"

John MacLean finished his telephone conversation and, replacing the receiver, turned round with a strange look on his face.

"What's up, Dad?" Neil asked.

"That was Jimmy MacFarlane on the phone," his father answered. "Apparently, some jokers have been making crop circles in the fields round about his farm and he asked me if I'd mind staying out all night with him and his men. They want to catch the people who are making them and as there's a lot of ground to cover, they need to rope in everyone they can to help."

"Crop circles," Clara queried, "in Scotland?"

"I've heard about them down south but not here," Mrs MacLean agreed.

"He really wants to nab them," her husband continued. "He's had a few fields done already and can't afford to lose another crop."

"Well," Janet advised, "if you're going to be scrabbling about in cornfields in the middle of the night, you'd better look out some old gear."

"Can I come as well, Dad?" Neil asked excitedly.

"He'd be another pair of eyes," his mother nodded her agreement.

John MacLean didn't answer immediately, however.

"There's something else, Dad, isn't there?" Clara said shrewdly. "I can tell by your face."

Mrs MacLean looked at her husband in surprise. "What on earth's the matter, John?" she asked. "Why shouldn't Neil go with you? He's old enough now."

"It's the crop circles," he replied. "Apparently, some reporters from *The Berwickshire News* went out to the farm to write an article about them and, of course, took photographs and ..."

"Well?" asked Neil.

"When they examined them it turned out that they were nothing like the crop circles you get in England. These are made up of pentagrams and other magic symbols. They seem to suspect witchcraft ..."

"Witches again ..." Clara's mouth went dry but her eyes gleamed excitedly.

Her mother, however, looked at her husband in dismay. More witches!

"Right, Dad," Neil said determinedly. "I'm definitely coming with you tonight and I'm going to wear my firestone."

"I'll lend you mine, Dad," Clara offered immediately, her hands rising to unclasp the thin chain that held her firestone. "If there are witches around then you'll want to be able to see them."

As she fastened the firestone round her father's neck, Neil moved over to the window and stared outside. Clara's witch must be long gone, he thought, but still he scanned the sky, hoping to see the black shape of a witch on a broomstick.

Minutes later, Clara moved up behind him, knowing what he was looking for. "Can you see anything?" she asked hopefully.

Neil shook his head. "Not a thing," he answered.

"We could go outside and poke around a bit," suggested Clara. "After all, my witch must have been pretty close to the house to come wandering in like that."

"You haven't got your firestone on, though," he objected.

"Never mind," she said as they headed for the front door, "you can tell me if you see anything."

A strong wind tugged at Clara's hair as they left the house, making her wish that she'd worn a jacket but, despite the cold, they walked together down to the clump of trees that bordered the little stream that ran through a corner of the garden.

It was there that Neil gripped Clara's arm. "Don't look in the trees," he whispered, his voice tight with excitement. "There are witches there. They're not dressed in black, like the one we saw in the house, though. This lot are in grey and, you know, I think Mum was right about them — they *do* seem to be looking for something."

They felt the wind strengthen as they entered the copse where the witches, intent on their task, moved from tree to tree on their broomsticks, delving deep into broken trunks and kicking aside piles of leaves.

Pretending that they couldn't see them, Neil picked up a stone and threw it idly into the stream but all the time he was watching them from the corner of his eye. The witches, however, safe in the knowledge that they were invisible, ignored them completely and it was only when Neil heard his mother's voice calling them inside that he grasped Clara's arm.

"Come on," he whispered, "I don't know what they're looking for but we'd better leave them to it."

Clara nodded, her eyes alight with excitement as she met Neil's glance. It looked as though life in the country wasn't going to be half as dull as they'd expected ...

5. Magic at midnight

The luminous hands of Neil's watch showed that it was well after ten before it got truly dark. He shifted uneasily in his hiding place at the edge of the wheat field wishing he'd chosen somewhere more comfortable for cover than a break in a hedge that seemed full of sharp, stabbing twigs that kept tangling in his hair. Not only that, he thought, rubbing a painful sting on his hand, there seemed to be an awful lot of nettles about.

Knowing that he was just going to have to put up with it, he sighed, hugged his knees to his chest and looking round, marvelled at the difference that nightfall made. The comfortable outline of hills, trees and the faraway glimpse of a country road running between stone dykes had long since melted away and he felt suddenly alone as the darkness deepened.

Time passed slowly. Waiting, he thought, was *the* most boring occupation and the feeling of tense excitement he'd felt when he and his dad had arrived was beginning to evaporate. The farmer had been brief in his directions. He'd already paired everyone off and as they'd moved away in different directions to their allotted posts, Neil wondered where he'd be put. He'd no idea where the Three Acre field was or Broad Meadow, where his father had been sent, but his ears pricked up at the mention of a place called Witches' Wood. More witches, he thought interestedly ...

"You, me and Robbie will cover the Home Field," Jimmy MacFarlane said to Neil when all the men had left. "It's the one nearest to the farmhouse. I want to be around if anyone's caught!"

Neil found himself a space in the hedge at the top of the field and watched as Robbie disappeared downhill into a fringe of trees near the road. Jimmy, himself, settled down near the gate where a huge combine harvester loomed in the fading light.

Trying to stay alert, Neil peered into the surrounding darkness but the huge field of wheat was only ever visible when the pale light of the moon appeared fitfully through the clouds. He looked again at the gleaming dial of his watch. Only half an hour had passed but it seemed like ages.

It was just when Neil had decided that nothing at all was going to happen that he heard a strange swishing noise. So low was it at first that he hardly noticed it but as it grew louder and closer, he sat up, excitement thrilling through him. There was no wind and yet the noise was that of rustling corn. Peering anxiously into the darkness, he couldn't see a thing and sat for a moment, undecided. It'd be awful if he started a false alarm. Better, he thought, to tell the farmer.

Getting quietly to his feet, he left his hiding place carefully and walking through soft patches of nettles made his way silently towards the gate. "Mr MacFarlane," he whispered. The darkness was absolute and there didn't seem to be anyone there. "Mr MacFarlane," he whispered again, louder this time. Still no one.

The wood of the gate felt rough under his hands and he wondered frantically what to do. If he shouted, he'd scare the people off and yet he couldn't tackle them on his own. Maybe Mr MacFarlane had gone into the farmhouse ...

Neil was halfway over the gate when the moon appeared from among the clouds, lighting the cornfield in its silvery gleam. He froze and, moving slowly so as not to attract attention, turned to see if he could see how many people were in the field; for the swishing, swooshing noise was now quite distinct.

As his eyes scanned the scene, he choked back a gasp of surprise for as far as he could see, there was no one there at all. The moonlight lit the field quite clearly and from his perch on the gate, he could see over its entire expanse. And it was scary; for although there was no one there, the wheat was alive with movement, swaying gently in places as though involved in some elaborate dance. It moved and dipped and flattened itself with no one there to touch it — no one that he could see, at any rate. Neil's mouth went dry as the corn beside the gate started to move and form fantastic shapes ...

And there are no witches, he thought, suddenly. There are no witches. I'm wearing my firestone and I'd see them if there were. This is magic ...

Hastily he clambered over the top of the gate and ran to the farmhouse. To his relief, he met the farmer coming out of the door.

"What's up, Neil? Is there someone in the field?"

Neil shook his head. "There's no one in the field," he whispered, his voice shaking with excitement. "The crop's moving on its own ..."

Jimmy MacFarlane heard the alarm in Neil's voice and grasped him reassuringly by the arm. "Calm down, laddie," he whispered. "Let's go and see."

As they approached the gate, however, the moon sailed behind the clouds once more and the blackness of night covered the field.

"If you come into the field you can see where the crop's been flattened," Neil whispered urgently, for he didn't want Jimmy MacFarlane to think him a silly town kid, afraid of the dark.

"I can do better than that, Neil," came the grim answer. "Just wait here."

MacFarlane turned to the huge bulk of the combine harvester that sat by the gate and, climbing into the cab, turned the engine on. The sound shattered the night and all the men in the surrounding fields looked up at the noise of it. They knew immediately what it was.

Neil had almost had a heart attack at the sudden roar of the engine. Then there was a blaze of light that lit up the whole area. Of course, thought Neil as the farmer jumped down, they need lights so that they can work at night.

He rushed to the gate and clambered up, standing to get a good view over the field. MacFarlane climbed up beside him and gasped as he realized

that the boy hadn't been imagining things at all.
The whole field was moving, and moving with a
purpose. He could see patterns taking shape before
his eyes without a soul being there to form them.

Neil was conscious of the rest of the farm
workers rushing up in a straggling crowd and
heard their cries of amazement as they, too,
watched the designs weave themselves among the
stalks of the wheat.

"Look!" Neil shouted in sudden horror. "Look!"
he pointed down the field to where the trees verged
on the road. "Robbie's going into the field!"

Robbie, fascinated by the movement of the
wheat, had moved from the shelter of the trees
into the crop itself. Gripped by a fearful sense
of dread, they watched him as he walked here
and there, grasping at the stalks of wheat as
they whipped themselves into sweeping curves or
flattened themselves to the earth.

"Get him out of there, Jimmy," John MacLean
said urgently, pushing his way through the
farmhands to the gate, "now, at once."

Neil looked at his father in astonishment and
then, as his firestone turned suddenly heavy,
understood his concern. There was big magic
around. Magic that he had never known before. He
gritted his teeth hard and clenched his fists to stop
himself gasping at the pain of it. His firestone! It
was so ... dreadfully ... heavy! Sweat beaded his
forehead as he fought an all consuming urge to
throw himself to the ground and bury himself deep
in the earth.

"Get yourself out of there, Robbie," Jimmy

MacFarlane bawled down the length of the field. "Right now, do you hear me!"

It was too late. They watched in horror as Robbie seemed to straighten and stretch before crumpling to the ground, disappearing from view into the waving wheat.

Some of the men made to clamber over the gate to run to his rescue but John MacLean's voice stopped them short.

"Wait," he said, in a voice of iron. "It's not over yet." And although he had no authority over them whatsoever, every man fell back and obeyed.

Neil felt like screaming. His firestone seemed to be dragging him to the ground. He felt his father's hand grip his arm strongly and knew that he, too, was struggling to stay upright. Then, suddenly, just as the intricate pattern was completed and the wheat stopped swaying, the pressure eased. Neil gulped and straightened thankfully, conscious that Jimmy MacFarlane was watching him strangely.

"Look! What's that light?" one of the men shouted, pointing to a darkened area away from the harvester's blazing lights.

"It's not the harvester," another agreed.

"Turn the lights out," MacFarlane shouted to one of the men who'd been watching the field from the cab of the machine.

The dazzling lights went out and as their eyes adjusted to the sudden darkness they were able to see the strange yellow glow that bathed the field. Neil stiffened and looked up at his father.

Someone from the world of magic was watching the field through a crystal ball.

6. Plots and plans

"The Earth Witches are making a great show of mourning my daughter's death," Lord Jezail remarked, indicating the intricate patterns wrought in the cornfield. "Have I miscounted, or does that make seven of them in all?"

"It does, milord," Count Vassili bowed his head and looked suitably solemn as the eye of crystal travelled slowly over the field.

Lord Jezail scowled. "Is that all you have to say?" he snapped.

Vassili eyed his master in some surprise. "But, surely the witches have done more than is required, milord," he pointed out after a moment's hesitation. "The Queen of the Earth Witches is a relative, after all," he pointed out diplomatically, "and it's natural that she would want to honour Lady Merial's memory."

"Maritza! Honour her memory!" Lord Jezail almost spat, "when she was as mad as fire at not getting the talisman!"

"But she *was* her cousin," Vassili pointed out, "and it's understandable that she'd expect to inherit it ..."

"If Merial wasn't going to leave the talisman to the witches then she should have sent it straight back to me!" Jezail muttered angrily. "She's made a mess of the whole affair!"

"Don't I know it," the count said feelingly, for keeping tabs on the witches was proving an absolute nightmare."

Lord Jezail drew his cloak round him and flung himself back in his vast chair. "Well, we can't give up now," he said petulantly. "We must be ready to take it from the witches whenever they find it! They must never be allowed to keep it."

Count Vassili listened with a sinking heart, knowing that he would probably moan on about it for the rest of the night. Finding the talisman would only be the start for Lord Jezail nursed many grudges, both real and imagined. Indeed, there were occasions when Vassili thought that his master was more than slightly mad. He'd once boasted about a hex he'd put on Prince Casimir and Prince Kalman when they'd visited Ashgar. Vassili shuddered at the thought. Indeed he'd been so disturbed by it that he'd almost decided to return to his father's estate at Trollsberg. Then there had been the disastrous Firestar affair when the whole world of magic had been put at risk. Not for the first time, he wondered if the Lords of the North had ever suspected anything ...

Lord Jezail looked at him suspiciously. "Very quiet all of a sudden, aren't you," he snapped.

"Milord ..." Count Vassili's heels clicked together as he bowed low, his blue eyes lifting to meet the hard, black stare of his master. Cold eyes, devoid of feeling; they were the shade of blue that one sometimes glimpses in the depths of ice: the eyes of a wolf.

Lord Jezail held his gaze and calmed himself. Vassili was generally so agreeable that he tended to forget that he was of the Onegin, the wolf people, who lived in the very north of Ashgar near the Russian border. Vassili came from quite a distinguished family of magicians and although his parents had sent him to Stara Zargana as an apprentice, his magic had, somehow, never seemed to amount to much ...

This seeming lack of talent was actually deliberate on Vassili's part as he had been quick to realize that Lord Jezail disliked competition of any sort. And it suited him to stay and browse through the vast library of magic books that, until his arrival, had lain untouched for centuries in the library of the citadel.

His master tapped the arm of his chair with restless fingers, his mind still on the talisman. "Merial must have hidden it well," he muttered discontentedly. "I really thought the witches would have found it by now."

Vassili sighed, for although his master spent the odd ten minutes studying the crystal, the tedious job of monitoring the witches had fallen mostly to him and he was heartily sick of it. "The trouble is, milord, that the witches aren't really all that bright," he pointed out. "They're looking in the most ridiculous places. The Wind Witches are searching the trees and bushes, the Earth Witches the rabbit holes and the Snow Witches are having to merge with birds and animals to do their work!

Quite frankly, if they go on at this rate, it'll take them *years* to find it."

"Years?" Jezail looked startled.

Vassili smiled ruefully. "Well, maybe not years," he admitted, "but the truth is, milord, that at the moment they're just wasting their time!"

Lord Jezail sat back in his huge, carved chair pondering Vassili's words and, eyeing his aide speculatively, looked suddenly thoughtful. It was a look that Vassili knew well and his expression became wary.

Lord Jezail's eyes gleamed. "All this is taking too long," he said, gesturing towards the crystal. "I'm too old to search for it myself and I've no intention of waiting for years until the witches find it. There's only one thing for it, Vassili! *You* will have to go and look for me!"

Vassili bowed and tried not to look surprised. The relief was enormous. To go to Scotland *on his own*! It was by no means the nightmare scenario he'd envisaged. Nevertheless, it was polite to protest and his voice was concerned as urged his master to accompany him.

"The change would do you good, milord," he pointed out, "and you could always stay with the MacArthurs or the Lords of the North?" He said this, knowing perfectly well that while his master might agree to staying with the MacArthurs, he would never go anywhere near Morven.

Lord Jezail looked at him arrogantly. "I've no wish to stay with either the Lords of the North or the MacArthurs," he said sharply. "You will go on your own and bring me back the talisman."

"It won't be easy, milord," Vassili protested somewhat anxiously. "After all, the witches have had no luck so far and quite frankly, I might not do much better. Er ... don't you have *any* idea where your daughter might have hidden it?" he enquired.

"None whatsoever," his master said unhelpfully, "and from the way the witches are setting about it, it would seem that they haven't a clue either," he muttered, turning once more to the crystal ball. "The only sensible thing they did was search Merial's house from top to bottom. Maritza, though," Lord Jezail continued, "might be on to something. I told you, didn't I? She's taken a job at Netherfield, the school Merial used to work in. It's an old building so there must be plenty of hiding places."

"That's a possibility," Vassili nodded, looking suddenly interested. "How big is the school?"

"See for yourself ... There it is." Jezail tilted the eye of the crystal to reveal a sprawling, turreted building that stood in its own grounds amid trees and playing fields.

"Maritza might well be on to something there," Vassili admitted, looking suddenly hopeful. "Could you arrange for them to need a ... a German teacher, perhaps?"

Lord Jezail looked at him sourly. "If that's what you want ..."

Count Vassili nodded. "It would be ideal, for as a member of staff I'd have access to all parts of the school. And let's just say that I have a feeling that Maritza *might* know something that the others don't," he added shrewdly. "Your daughter *was*, after all, her cousin."

7. Surprising news

"The MacLeans are on their way," Jaikie said, looking up from a crystal ball that showed the green slopes of Arthur's Seat and the Ranger's cottage that lay just inside the great gates of Holyrood Park. "They've just left their cottage, and Neil and Clara are with them."

The MacArthur nodded and Arthur, the great red dragon that curled beside his chair, blew a cloud of smoke down his nostrils that set everybody coughing. Like the MacArthurs, he was very fond of the Park Ranger and his family and had been devastated to hear that they were leaving their cottage to live in the Borders. Over the years they'd had some very exciting adventures together and they'd all got used to having the children drop in on their magic carpets just for a chat.

"Give over, Arthur," Archie muttered, flapping his hands. "It isn't *all* that long since you've seen Neil and Clara."

"It is," Arthur disagreed. "It's weeks since they left."

"Well, here they are now," Hamish announced a few minutes later, rising to his feet as four magic carpets soared from a side tunnel into the vast, richly-decorated cavern that lay inside Arthur's

Seat. The carpets swooped in, one after the other, to hover beside a raised dais where the MacArthur sat, a small but regal figure, on a huge, elaborately carved chair piled high with cushions.

Neil and Clara slipped off their carpets with the ease of long practice and after a hasty greeting to the MacArthur, ran over to the dragon.

The carpets dipped gently and flew to the side of the cavern where they rolled themselves up against the wall; ready and waiting until called again.

"It's grand to see you looking so well," the MacArthur smiled. "Country life seems to be agreeing with you. How are you getting on in your new house?"

John MacLean looked at him shrewdly. "Not too well," he admitted, "but I think you probably know that already," he added with a smiling glance at the crystal. "That's why we've come. We need your advice."

"You mean about the witches?" the MacArthur said.

"Yes, about the witches," the Ranger agreed, settling himself comfortably in his chair. "One of them gave Clara a real scare."

Janet looked at the MacArthur expectantly, waiting for his reply, for he was just the person to solve what she referred to as "the witch problem".

Neil and Clara, still chatting to Arthur, dragged cushions forward to sit alongside Archie, Hamish and Jaikie who were lounging casually against the dragon's massive side. Clara looked over at her father and nodded at his words. "She wasn't a snow witch," she said, tucking her long, brown hair behind her ears. "*They* are beautiful, but this one was really ugly; she had a hooked nose and her clothes were black."

"She was an Earth Witch, then," Jaikie said knowledgeably. "The Earth Witches wear black and the Wind Witches wear grey."

Grey! Neil and Clara eyed one another in quick understanding. It must have been Wind Witches that they had seen searching the trees near their house.

"Really?" Janet MacLean said, looking over at him in surprise. "I didn't know there were different kinds of witches."

Archie nodded. "They're a jealous lot," he remarked, "always squabbling."

The MacArthur nodded. "They don't get on with one another at all," he agreed. "We knew you'd be having problems with them the minute Merial died."

"You mean Muriel," the Ranger corrected him with a smile, "my sister-in-law."

"No, I don't," the MacArthur said with a sidelong glance at Archie, Hamish and Jaikie. He paused momentarily, well aware of the consternation he was about to cause. "I mean Lady Merial, daughter of Lord Jezail of Ashgar, one of the greatest magicians in Europe."

There was a blank silence as the MacLeans gawped, open-mouthed at this disclosure.

"You're ... you're not having us on, are you?" John MacLean said eventually in a voice that was little more than a whisper.

The MacArthur shook his head.

Neil and Clara glanced at one another; but while Neil looked as amazed as his parents, Clara became suddenly thoughtful. She had always been close to her aunt. They'd got on well together and if she really *was* a magician's daughter then that would explain quite a lot; for their conversations had often been about magic. It must have been about a year ago, she thought, when they'd been on a picnic. The others had gone for a walk but she had stayed behind to help clear up and her aunt had quizzed her about her firestone pendant. She remembered how she'd blushed when her aunt had called it a magic stone and then smiled at her in a most peculiar way as though she'd guessed at all her adventures with the MacArthurs. And there were the odd comments she sometimes made as well. "Did you know that witches," she'd once remarked, "can't cross running water. They have to use bridges." Yes, she thought, it was quite possible that Auntie Muriel had been a magician's daughter.

Still looking stunned, the Ranger searched his memory for details. "David met Muriel in Austria when he was on a skiing holiday," he said, running his hands through his hair. "I don't remember him ever calling her Merial, though," he added, a frown creasing his brow as he looked at the MacArthur. "According to him, her father disapproved of their marriage and more or less cut Merial off, there and then."

"Now we know why," his wife interrupted.

"Well, yes," John continued, "but having said that, it didn't seem to worry her. They came back to Scotland, settled in at Craiglaw House and were perfectly happy."

"She was lovely," added Janet, still sounding flabbergasted, "a thoroughly nice woman. I can't believe she had anything to do with witches or magic."

"Why did you say that we'd be having problems the minute she died?" Neil queried, remembering the MacArthur's opening remark.

"Ah," the MacArthur said, "that's where things start to get complicated. You see, Merial's father, Lord Jezail, doted on his daughter and when she was young, he gave her a magic talisman as a gift."

"What's a talisman?" Clara asked.

"It's a magic token. In this case, an engraved silver clasp that's worn round the arm. It not only protected Merial from hexes and spells but gave her control over the witches. They're spiteful, you see, and left to themselves they'd delight in calling up storms and the like — cspccially at harvest time when the farmers need good weather to bring in the crops."

"I never saw Muriel wearing anything like that," Janet mused thoughtfully. "Did you, John?"

Her husband shook his head.

"She probably kept it hidden in case you sensed its magic," the MacArthur said reasonably, "and you might have done, you know. After all, *she* knew that *you* wore firestones."

"She did?" They all looked at the MacArthur in complete astonishment.

"But ... she never said anything to any of us ..." Mrs MacLean looked completely bewildered.

"No, but she asked me about you all the same, and I think she was pleased to hear that you had helped us in so many ways." Seeing that Mrs MacLean was still upset, he added gently. "She might have found it easier to say nothing, Janet," and, as Mrs MacLean opened her mouth to disagree, he said quickly, "I know you might find it hard to accept but I think she'd have found explanations difficult. Anyway,' he pointed out, 'she knew that I would explain things to you afterwards."

"About the witches?"

The MacArthur nodded. "About the witches," he agreed. "The Earth Witches, that is, for the Queen of the Earth Witches was actually her cousin by marriage. She took Merial under her wing when she came to Scotland and that's how Merial joined the ranks of the Earth Witches. She used the talisman's magic well and more or less ruled with the queen. And because of their close relationship, the Queen of the Earth Witches quite naturally assumed that she would inherit the talisman when Merial died."

"You mean Merial left the talisman to someone else?" Janet asked.

"No, she didn't."

"What did she do with it, then?" queried Clara.

"That's the problem," gestured the MacArthur, unhappily. "She's hidden it somewhere. The witches are combing the countryside for it. They're searching houses, farms, fields and woods. Everywhere and anywhere that Merial might have visited."

"So that's why they were searching our house," Janet sounded grim. "It would be the first place they'd look."

The MacArthur nodded.

"Do they have anything at all to do with the crop circles that have been appearing?" Neil asked, sounding serious. "Dad and I saw one of them being made and there was no one in the field."

"Yes, that was the witches," the MacArthur nodded.

"Neil said that his firestone got really heavy," Clara added curiously.

"The witches would be working beneath the field," the MacArthur explained. "That's why his firestone was affected."

"One of the men went into the field while the circle was being made," the Ranger said. "He passed out but seemed okay when he came round afterwards. It was really weird. Everyone knew that something strange was going on. The newspapers are full of it and everyone in the countryside is nervous."

"Nervous?" echoed Neil. "Scared, you mean!"

"But why are the witches making crop circles anyway?" Janet asked.

"It's the custom," the MacArthur explained. "The witches made them as a ... a tribute to Merial. To honour her departure from this world. They couldn't let her passing go unnoticed, you know. She was a lady of importance in her own right."

"Someone was looking at the crop circle through a crystal," Neil said. "Dad and I recognized the light."

"Was it you, by any chance?" his father asked.

The MacArthur nodded his head. "Yes," he said, suddenly serious, "we were, of course, watching. As, I'm sure, were many others from the world of magic — including, I should imagine, her father, Lord Jezail."

8. Scarecrows

The poacher stood still and silent in the dark shadow of the trees, avoiding the slanting beams of moonlight that penetrated the leafy thickness of the wood. The quiet, rippling gurgle of the river sounded softly in the background as he glanced around, suddenly alert as he sensed that something was wrong. He turned his head slowly, this way and that, catching the breeze and the smell of the earth. After years of poaching the odd salmon from the Tweed, he'd developed a strong feeling for the land and knew the breath of the wood.

A strange unease gripped him. Maybe a gamekeeper on the prowl, he told himself, although he knew instinctively that it was nothing so ordinary. Again he turned his head and tested the wind. Nothing, he thought, his eyes searching the trees. And yet he knew within himself that there was someone or something close by, watching him. Then he saw it, standing on a slight rise over to his left; a large dog with a rough, grey coat. Must be a stray, he thought, living in the wild, off rabbits and other small creatures. It stood still, watching him and as he met its cold, blue-eyed stare the friendly words that had risen to his lips, remained unspoken. A wolf! It was a wolf! He stood his ground, not daring to move and, heart thumping furiously, watched as the animal turned and loped off among the trees.

What *was* it about the wood, he wondered tensely, looking round searchingly. Fear still gripped him and the sight of the wolf had sent panic bubbling through his veins. Conscious of the hefty salmon he carried in a twist of rough sacking, he turned and moved stealthily through the trees towards his cottage. Treading softly and warily, he was conscious that all his senses were sharp, tense and alert; tuned into every small rustle of sound and every movement of the trees.

It was when he reached the edge of the wood that he saw him, a still figure in the shadowy moonlight; the uniformed figure of a policeman leaning casually against a tree. Relief flooded through him. A copper! Thank goodness for that! In the state he was in, he'd half expected some strange daemon or spectre of the wood. Nevertheless, he groaned inwardly, knowing that the game was up; to be caught poaching was a serious offence.

The still figure, however, made no move towards him until it dawned on him that there was something decidedly odd about the policeman. Moving closer, he reached into his coat pocket and, taking out a powerful torch, shone the beam into the man's face. He gasped in horror and swore aloud as he saw the figure clearly — for it wasn't a man at all, but a scarecrow dressed as a policeman; the painted turnip face and straw body looking remarkably life-like in the shadowy glimmer of the moonlight. Kids, he thought furiously, angry at the scare he'd had. Some kids must have brought it into the wood.

To his dismay, he found that he was more seriously disturbed than he'd thought. His hands were shaking violently and in a sudden fit of revulsion, he hurled the stuffed figure, in a swinging tangle of arms and legs, into the bushes and hurried towards the scatter of trees that fringed the wood. Making his way through them, he clambered over a wire fence, jumped a ditch and reached the path that led to his cottage. He strode along swiftly, anxious now to get home but it was only as he drew closer to his house that he saw them; dark figures prowling round the old barn at the back.

Moving quickly, he dumped his fish by the gate and taking a short cut through the field, crept up on them. What he couldn't figure out was what they were after, for there was nothing in the barn worth stealing; even the old tractor didn't work.

As he got nearer, he took the flashlight from his pocket and clicking it on, lit up the stooping, searching figures that seemed to be everywhere, poking about in all the corners.

He'd grabbed hold of the nearest one before his brain told him what his eyes had seen and it was then that he screamed in horror for it was not a man that he held in his grasp but a scarecrow. A scarecrow dressed as a cowboy with a painted bag as a face, straw arms and a body stuffed with what felt like rags. And it was alive.

*

"I stopped off at Norham to get the newspapers," John MacLean said to his wife as he came into the living room, "and the Mason's Arms is absolutely heaving with reporters."

"Is it this scarecrow business?" Janet queried, looking up from her sewing. "They've even had it on TV."

"Do you think it's the witches' doing?" Clara asked.

"Looks like it," her father replied.

"What's everyone saying?" Clara queried. "I mean, scarecrows coming to life is really something!"

"Seemingly, it all started last week during the Norham Scarecrow Festival. You know that each house makes its own scarecrow ..."

"They're marvellous," Janet added, threading a needle carefully. "I saw them last year when I was visiting Muriel."

"Well, at first they thought they had a practical joker in the village because one morning people woke up to find that the scarecrow in their garden wasn't the one they'd made. They got quite angry, especially when they found that the same thing had happened all over the village. And we're not talking about one or two scarecrows here, you know. Norham's a big place. Anyway, there was a good deal of bad-tempered muttering as people found their own scarecrows again and got themselves sorted out."

"And?" asked Clara curiously.

"Well, the next night, the same thing happened again, so they formed a committee to police the village at night, to see who was mucking them about."

"And did they catch anybody?"

"Well, no, they didn't," her father said. "Apparently, the entire committee fell asleep on the job."

"Fell asleep?" Mrs MacLean echoed incredulously.

Her husband nodded. "And once again all the scarecrows were sitting outside the wrong houses in the morning and," he shrugged, "nobody could understand how all that moving around could happen without at least one of the committee waking up."

"Well, that figures," Clara grinned.

"Mmm, I think they came in for a good deal of stick," her father nodded. "Of course, it's probably the witches' doing. I reckon they're using the scarecrows to help them search the countryside.

"There was some talk of a tramp hanging round the place as well; an old man with grey hair. Some people blamed him but most of them thought he wouldn't have had the strength. Then the local poacher arrived in the middle of it all, scared out of his mind. Said he'd seen a wolf down by the river and found scarecrows searching his barn. Live scarecrows! The countryside's buzzing with it!"

"I'd much rather have scarecrows than witches!" Mrs MacLean declared.

"They'd be stupid to come here again," Clara pointed out. "We're wearing our firestones and we'd see them the minute they appeared."

"I think the witches had already given the house a good going over before we even moved in," her father said thoughtfully. "I shouldn't worry. They'll be concentrating on other hiding places now."

"Good riddance," snapped Janet MacLean, finishing her sewing and biting off the thread.

"You know, I think I'll wear my firestone when I go to school," Clara said thoughtfully. "If there *are* any witches around, I want to be able to see them."

John MacLean looked at her thoughtfully. "You might well see witches at school," he warned. "Your aunt taught at Netherfield, remember? You never know, she might have hidden the talisman there."

"That's true," Mrs MacLean said, looking at Clara in sudden dismay. "I didn't think of that!"

9. Netherfield

"How was your first week then?" was their father's first question as they dumped their heavy bags in the boot of the 4x4. "Do you think you're going to like it?"

"It's great," Neil said, rushing round the car to grab the front seat. Clara made a face at him but opened the back door and clambered in, still feeling strange in the green blazer and kilt that formed the school uniform. She looked back at the imposing building, picking out her bedroom window in one of the four huge towers that stood at each corner of the building.

"Clara was homesick," Neil remarked as his father manoeuvred the car carefully through the mass of cars and buses in the car park.

"Were you, Clara?" her father said in surprise, looking at her in the rear-view mirror.

"The first few nights were a bit lonely," she admitted.

"Would you like to share with somebody?" her father questioned. "I'm sure it could be arranged. Your mum and I thought you'd like having a room to yourself."

Clara shook her head. "The other boarders are all primary kids. Anyway, I'm getting used to being on my own."

"You missed me, that's what it is," Neil grinned.

Clara promptly stuck her tongue out at him, loath to admit that, in actual fact, she *had* missed him!

"By the way, your mum plans to take you into Berwick tomorrow," their father interrupted before Clara could retaliate further. "We stopped there on our way down from Edinburgh to stock up with groceries and she saw a shop that sells posters; all your kind of stuff ... you know, pop stars, footballers ... that sort of thing. She thought you might like to buy some of them to put up in your room."

"Great!" Neil said, immediately diverted at the mention of footballers. "By the way, who's playing who tomorrow, Dad?"

Clara sat in the back of the car and as Neil and her father discussed football, watched the trees, hedges and fields slide by as they headed for home. By the time they reached Craiglaw House, she was feeling much better and seeing her mother, she smiled and waved as she scrambled out of the car. It's not fair to worry Mum, she thought, as she rushed forward to hug her.

"I've lit the fire in the living room," her mother said later. "I want to hear all about Netherfield. How you're coping with the lessons and what the teachers are like ..." she added, pushing the door open and switching on the light.

Clara settled herself on a stool by the fire and stretched out a hand to the blaze. The weather was getting colder by the day.

"Clara and I hardly ever see one another," she heard Neil say. "We're in different classes for a start ..."

"Yes, and the boys' bedrooms are in another tower altogether," Clara added.

"And what about school work?" queried her mother. "Are you managing to keep up?"

"Well, Maths and English are okay and apart from the teacher, I quite like Drama," Clara added, brightening at the thought. "Our year is putting on a play for Halloween, all about witches and stuff."

"I know," Neil nodded. "The rest of the seniors have been invited to watch the dress rehearsal. It was on the notice board this morning."

"It's just a pity Miss Markham's so awful," Clara said. "Nobody likes her; she's really strict. You *must* have seen her round the place, Neil," she looked at her brother enquiringly, "a real drama queen — tall, with black hair, black eyes and always *so* over the top about everything!"

"I think she's probably foreign," Neil said. "She signed the notice Maritza Markham."

"Could be," Clara said considering the matter. "She certainly doesn't *look* Scottish."

"And what about you, Neil?" interrupted his father.

"It's just German that's the problem," Neil said glumly. "All the others started it in primary so Clara and I have a lot of catching up to do."

"Do you have Mrs Weston for English?" his mother queried. "She's a short woman, fair hair and a bit absent-minded."

"Always losing her glasses," added Neil with a grin. "Yes, I do. She's my form mistress. She told me she knew Auntie Muriel."

"Mmm, they were close friends. Believe me, she isn't nearly as vague as she looks and if you have any problems, she's someone you can trust."

"Oops! I'm sorry, Clara," her father said, getting to his feet suddenly, "I almost forgot. A letter came for you while you were at school."

Clara looked startled. "A letter," she said in surprise, "for me?"

"I should have given it to you earlier," he added, taking a stamped envelope from the mantelpiece.

Her mother looked at it curiously. "It's from the lawyer," she said.

"Maybe Auntie Muriel's left you thousands of pounds," Neil grinned.

His father shook his head. "The estate's been settled," he said. "It can't be that."

"Open it then, Clara," Neil urged as she turned it over in her hand, 'don't keep us in suspense!"

"You open it, Dad," she said, handing it back to him, looking suddenly upset. "Please!"

Her father shrugged, slit the envelope open and took out a sheet of stiff paper and another, smaller envelope.

"Well, John?" his wife asked.

"How strange," he muttered, handing Clara the small envelope. "It's from the lawyer. He says that your aunt asked him to send you this letter, Clara ..."

"He's taken his time about it then, hasn't he?" Neil observed. "I mean, Auntie Muriel died a couple of months ago."

"He apologises for the delay," continued his father, "but your aunt instructed him to wait for two months before he sent it to you ..."

They all looked puzzled as Clara looked at the white envelope in her hand and opened it reluctantly. Why, she didn't know, although she was soon to find out. She just had a feeling that once it was opened, nothing would ever be quite the same again.

"Well, what does she say?" demanded Neil curiously.

"It isn't a letter," Clara said, her eyes scanning the sheet of paper and holding it out so that they could all see it. "It's some sort of riddle about ... about a talisman."

"A talisman!" echoed her mother. "Do you think it's the one the MacArthur was telling us about? The one the witches are looking for?"

Neil read the riddle swiftly. "Must be," he said, his eyes alight with excitement. "Good old Auntie Muriel! This must tell us where she hid it."

"Read it out, Neil," his mother said. "What does it say?"

"No," Clara said suddenly, grabbing the paper from Neil and folding it in two, "that isn't a good idea. Somebody might be watching us ... through a crystal," she explained. "The witches perhaps!"

"Do witches have crystals?" Neil asked curiously as they all looked round apprehensively. "I thought it was only magicians."

"Nonsense," her mother said dismissively, holding out her hand, "Who would be interested in us?"

Clara looked sceptical but handed her the folded sheet of paper. "Let's not take the risk," she muttered. "It ought to be okay if you cover it with your hand."

"Then she won't be able to read it, stupid!" Neil butted in.

"Neil," his father said warningly.

Mrs MacLean read the riddle and folding the paper again, passed it to her husband.

The Talisman

Beside the firelight
Lies your treasure
A talisman from ages past
Cast in silver, steeped in magic
Keep it safe and use it well
Bind it to you, meet its challenge
Until it's time to pass it on
Look to Morven's Lords for guidance
Let their wisdom rule your choice

"Shhhh!" Clara said urgently, as everyone's eyes automatically focused on the fireplace, 'don't say anything out loud."

"You're being ridiculous, Clara," her mother said. "Who would watch us?"

"Well ... you never know," Neil chipped in, his eyes scanning the room warily.

"I don't want any witches in the house again," her mother said, alarmed at the thought.

John MacLean nodded agreement. "Nor do I," he said. "Look, why don't we all memorize the riddle and once we've done it, Clara can hide the paper somewhere safe."

"And when you're hiding it," Neil advised, "hide it in the dark. Then if anybody *is* watching you through a crystal, you'll know, 'cos you'll see the light."

"Good thinking, Neil," his father said approvingly.

Mrs MacLean moved to the door and switched off the central light, leaving the room lit only by flickering firelight and the glow of a table lamp. "Well," she said with a sigh of relief, "obviously no one is watching us. We'll keep it this way until we learn the rhyme, shall we?"

Clara spread it out on the coffee table and they took it in turns to memorize the riddle. It wasn't long, nor was it difficult to remember.

"It doesn't really tell us very much, though, does it?" Neil said after five minutes. "Apart from the obvious, that is," he added, looking pointedly at the fireplace.

"Come on," Clara said, folding the paper briskly. "Let's have a look and see if we can see anything strange about it." The fireplace, however, seemed perfectly normal. It was big, admittedly, but there didn't seem to be any loose bricks.

Neil, ignoring the heat, twisted his head and tried to peer up the chimney itself but his father drew him back. "The riddle says 'by the firelight', Neil," he pointed out. "It doesn't mention the chimney. Anyway, we had the chimney sweep in last week and I was here all the time, watching. There were no secret packages tucked away up the chimney, I assure you!"

"It certainly doesn't look as though this is the fireplace we're looking for," Mrs MacLean agreed.

"Actually, it could be *any* fireplace, *anywhere*," John MacLean mused. "Possibly at Netherfield," he added, his expression brightening. "There's a huge fireplace in the big hall."

Mrs MacLean looked at Clara apprehensively. "You didn't see any witches while you were there, did you?" she asked.

Clara shook her head. "I didn't have the chance," she admitted. "Jewellery's against the rules so I couldn't wear my firestone. Neither could Neil."

"Mind you, we *could* wear them under our uniforms," Neil pointed out. "No one would ever know."

"That's true," Clara agreed, "as long as we don't have P.E. or anything."

They pondered the riddle for some time but in the end gave up.

"I can't make it out at all," Neil said exasperatedly, pushing the paper to one side. "As far as I can see, it doesn't give us any clue as to where the fireplace actually is!"

It was later that night when they were going upstairs to their bedrooms that Neil had a bright idea. "You know, Clara," he whispered, "we could have a good look at the fireplace in the school hall when everyone's asleep. I mean, nobody would be about at night, would they?"

Clara nodded in agreement. "What about meeting at midnight in the entrance hall, then? The witching hour!" she grinned.

10. Ill-met by moonlight

Clara almost knocked her bedside lamp over as she grabbed for her alarm as it went off in a jangle of noise that set her pulses racing. Convinced that she must have woken at least half of the school, she switched it off hastily and sat up straight in bed, listening frantically. Nothing, however, stirred and she released her breath in a sigh of relief as she looked round the room. It was becoming more familiar now and the posters she'd stuck up on the walls looked really cool.

She slipped quickly into some dark trousers and pulled on a top, before twisting her long hair back into a ponytail so that it didn't flop over her face.

It was then that she took a grey, dull-looking ring from the third finger of her right hand and transferred it to the ring finger of her left hand. She looked at her reflection in the long mirror fastened to the back of her bedroom door. It showed her room and nothing else. She was invisible. She smiled softly as she switched it back again. The magic rings were for emergencies only and really, there was no need for them at this time of night. No one would be around to see them and they'd be as quiet as mice.

Excitement thrilled through her as she thought of the adventure to come. Would they find the talisman in the hall fireplace? She hoped they would for otherwise the possibilities were endless. Most country houses had big, open fireplaces and if there was another clue in the riddle, she had yet to find it.

Cautiously, she opened her bedroom door and holding onto the banister made her way carefully down the spiral stair, grateful for the moonlight.

The school seemed totally deserted and although she crept quietly along at first, her confidence gradually grew and by the time she reached the long corridor that led to the main staircase, she was striding along, thoroughly enjoying the adventure.

She stopped abruptly, however, when a black shadow suddenly swept across the stretch of windows that lined the corridor. An owl, she thought, flying in front of the moon? No, surely it was too big for an owl. She turned and, looking out to see what sort of bird it was, clapped a hand over her mouth to stifle a scream. There, flying in the darkness above the grounds of the school was a witch; a witch on a broomstick.

Heart racing frantically, she stood rooted to the spot, unable to take her eyes off the shadowy figure that was growing ever smaller as it headed out towards the main road and the hills beyond. She was only roused from her trance by a whispered voice.

"Clara," she heard Neil call from the end of the corridor. "Clara? Where are you?"

Clara turned. She had forgotten all about meeting Neil. "Neil," she choked.

He ran lightly up to her. "What's the matter?" he hissed. "Clara! What's wrong?"

"Neil," she said, grabbing him urgently, "you'll never guess what I've just seen! I ... I was on my way to meet you and ... and something flew across the window. You're never going to believe this but ... it was a witch," she said, "a witch on a broomstick!"

"A witch!" Neil's eyes narrowed as he strode to the window and looked out over the moonlit grounds. "There's nothing there now," he observed.

"I know," she whispered impatiently. "But that isn't what's freaking me out! Listen to me, Neil! I reckon she came from *inside* the school. I'm sure she did; from one of those windows over there."

"I think that's the staff living quarters," Neil said, peering out.

"You know what it means, don't you?" she said in a whisper.

"Yes," Neil's voice was hard as he answered, "It means that one of the staff is a witch! Look," he said, "what if we just have a quick peep at the fireplace in the big hall. If we do it now, then at least it'll be over and done with — and it won't take long, either."

"Okay," Clara whispered, taking a deep breath. "Let's go!"

They slipped silently down the main staircase and over the stone-flagged floor towards the hall. For a moment, Neil thought it might be locked but the door handle turned quite easily and, shivering with excitement, they crept inside.

Moonlight lit up row upon row of chairs, set out for assembly the next morning, but they only had eyes for the massive fireplace at the far end of the hall.

It was so big that when they clambered inside, Clara found she could stand upright under the chimney. But although they went over it carefully, there was nothing to show that anything had been hidden there.

Clara looked disappointed as she stepped back and shook her head. "There doesn't seem to be anything here," she whispered.

"What about the library?" Neil said, pursing his lips thoughtfully. "It has a big fireplace in it as well."

Clara nodded. She had recovered from the shock of seeing the witch and wasn't the least bit tired. Besides which, she was quite enjoying their midnight adventure. The library, however, was further away than she'd thought and she quickly lost track of where she was. "Is it much further?" she whispered.

"Just along here," he replied.

They both stopped, however, when they reached the heavy, panelled door, looking at it uncertainly. It was ajar. Someone was in the library! At this time of night? Who could it possibly be? Neil leant forward quietly. "Change your ring over," he breathed in her ear, "just in case ..."

Clara nodded and promptly disappeared as she changed her magic ring to the other hand. She couldn't see Neil now and, reaching out, felt for his arm as he pushed the door open a little further so that they could slip inside.

At first they couldn't see anybody. Maybe, Neil thought, the door had just been left open by accident; but then again, perhaps not.

Don't let there be a witch, Clara was thinking. Please, don't let there be a witch.

Walking silently, they moved from aisle to aisle, slipping between the high bookcases, searching each alcove for the intruder. Then they saw him and Clara breathed a sigh of relief. Thank goodness, she thought. It wasn't a witch, after all; it was one of the staff.

Neil froze, recognizing the German teacher, Herr von Grozny. At first he thought, quite naturally, that the man had come to the library to look for a book but this was not the case. Not the case at all. The man was obviously searching for something, his hands moving swiftly and methodically behind the rows of books.

Neil pulled on Clara's hand and they moved closer to him. It was a mistake. They realized it the minute the man stiffened. His head lifted and he seemed to sniff the air before whirling round, his pale blue eyes searching the room.

Neil couldn't believe it. He knew they were there! Heart beating fast, he tugged on Clara's hand.

She didn't need to be told. They had to get away. Nerves tense they moved steadily backwards, very gently, step by step. Herr von Grozny, however, made for the door at a run and Neil's heart sank as he realized that the room, although huge, was a trap. There was only one way in and out.

Just as Von Grozny reached the door, however, one of the school janitors appeared; a stooped, elderly man with greying hair.

"Is anything the matter, Herr von Grozny?" he asked.

There was a curious, strained silence. Von Grozny straightened and his eyes flashed coldly blue as they met those of the old man. Such was the tension between them that Clara gripped Neil's hand hard.

"No," Von Grozny said slowly, "I came down to look for a book."

"You didn't find it, then?" the janitor said, observing his empty hands.

"Er ... no, I didn't." He looked at his watch. "My goodness, it's much later than I thought. My apologies. I'll look for it again tomorrow."

"That's fine then, Sir," the janitor smiled. "Off you go and I'll lock up."

Von Grozny shot the man a furious, somewhat baffled, look before striding swiftly away down the corridor. The janitor, however, seemed in no hurry to leave. He left the door standing wide open as he inspected the library to see that everything was intact and by the time he returned, Neil and Clara were long gone.

11. Of wolves and witches

Once they had escaped from the library, Neil and Clara had hurriedly agreed not to wear their firestones in class in case the witch, whoever she was, sensed their magic. Still trembling with shock, their one idea was to reach the safety of their rooms in case von Grozny was still prowling the corridors. There was barely time to say anything else and for the rest of the week both had waited eagerly for Friday to come so that they could discuss what had happened.

"We've lots to tell you," Neil said to his mother as he and Clara entered the kitchen. Mrs MacLean, however, busy unpacking groceries and feeling more than slightly flustered, hardly heard him.

Frowning as she scanned the assortment of food that lay on the work surface, she sighed as she handed Clara a carton of milk to put in the fridge. "Living between two houses isn't a picnic," she observed irritably. "I *always* seem to manage to forget something!"

It was only later that evening when they'd had dinner and were settled round the fire that Mrs MacLean remembered Neil's words. "You said that you had lots to tell us when you came in. Did something happen at school?"

Neil told them with Clara chipping in occasionally.

"You saw a witch — on a broomstick?" her mother said in disbelief.

"I was wearing my firestone," Clara nodded. "That's why I could see her. She'd be invisible to everyone else, of course."

"What worries me most about the whole affair is that Herr von Grozny *knew* we were in the library," interrupted Neil, "we were wearing our rings and only magic people would sense that we were there, you know."

Clara nodded. "I had German yesterday," she said with a sudden shiver, "and I was scared to look him in the face."

Neil nodded. "We're all dead quiet in his class," he admitted. "But he's a superb teacher. I can speak quite a lot of German already, you know. It's ..."

"It's what, Neil?" his father queried, looking at him in surprise, for Neil had stopped abruptly.

"I was going to say," Neil swallowed, "that it was ... almost magical how easily I was picking it up."

Clara looked at him, gathering his meaning. "Yeah," she said thoughtfully, "I've been finding it dead easy as well. Do you think he is? I mean, using magic to get us to learn?"

Neil nodded.

"Maybe we should go up to Edinburgh tomorrow," Mrs MacLean said uneasily as she looked across the room at her husband. "I'd be a lot happier if the MacArthur knew what was going on."

Her husband nodded. "You're right," he agreed, "but it'll have to be next weekend. You're forgetting that the builder's dropping by tomorrow with some tile samples."

"Next week will be okay," Neil nodded, "and you don't need to drive down to collect us," he added. "We can get the school bus to drop us at Berwick Station and catch the train up to Edinburgh."

"Great," Clara said, her eyes shining at the thought of an unexpected train journey, "and you never know, maybe the MacArthur will be able to solve Auntie Muriel's riddle as well," she added.

The MacArthur raised his eyebrows when he read Clara's riddle and, handing it to Hamish, Jaikie and Archie, looked at her thoughtfully. The talisman, as he had told her, was a powerful object of magic and what the Lords of the North would say at such a turn of events, he wasn't quite sure. Arthur, the great dragon, curled contentedly beside the MacArthur's chair, listened with the others as Neil and Clara recounted what had happened at school the week before and, when they'd finished, said in his hissing, dragon voice. "Lady Merial has given you a dangerous task, Clara."

Everyone nodded and looked questioningly at the MacArthur.

"We were hoping that you might be able to work out the riddle," John MacLean said hopefully.

The MacArthur shook his head as did Hamish, Jaikie and Archie. "I wish I could, but I'm as baffled as you are," he admitted.

"I was hoping that Kitor might be here," Clara said, looking round for the crow that had shared many of their adventures. "I thought it might be a good idea if he and Cassia could come to school and stay with us for a while. The grounds are huge and there are lots of trees around for them to hide in. They'd be able to keep a look out for the witch and tell us where she goes and everything."

"That's not a problem," the MacArthur smiled. "They'll be back soon and you can sort it out then. I'm sure they'd love to stay with you."

"That's a great idea, Clara," Neil said, sitting up straight on his cushion. "They could take messages between us, as well," he added, looking at the MacArthur. "We hardly see one another at school," he explained, "and we need to keep in touch."

"It's a pity that we're too far away from Edinburgh to call our magic carpets all the time," Clara said. "They'd be ideal for exploring the countryside."

Hamish and Jaikie looked at one another and then at the MacArthur. "Er ... there are always the broomsticks," Jaikie offered tentatively.

"Broomsticks?" Neil and Clara repeated together, looking at him in amazement. "What broomsticks?"

"The Snow Witches' broomsticks that we used when we were trying to get the Sultan's Crown from Prince Kalman. We brought them back from Ardray, remember?"

"Yes," nodded Clara, "that's right, we did ... I remember now."

"Well, they're here," Jaikie said. "Hamish and I saw them just the other day. They're in one of the store rooms."

"Brilliant," Clara said, looking eagerly at the MacArthur. "That would mean that Neil and I could meet up at night and nobody would know."

"Hmmm," said the MacArthur, looking doubtful.

"We have our magic rings as well," Neil reminded him, "no one would see us."

"It's not that," Archie broke in, suddenly concerned. "The witches are a vicious lot and they have some really nasty hexes up their sleeves. You've got to be careful."

Seeing the look of apprehension that crossed Mrs MacLean's face, the MacArthur beckoned Neil and Clara forward.

"Come here a minute," he said, "and give me your firestones."

Lifting their hands to their necks, Neil and Clara unfastened the chains that held their glowing firestones. The MacArthur rose to his feet and putting them on a small side table, hexed them. The flash of light that streaked from his fingers made them jump, even though they were expecting it, and they watched with fascinated eyes as, for a second, the firestones glowed with a luminous brilliance. It wasn't often that they saw the MacArthur use his magic and they were impressed.

It was only when the light faded that the MacArthur handed them back and as Clara fastened her firestone round her neck, she felt its magic spark against her.

"You said that the teacher in the library sensed that you were there, even though he couldn't see you and had no way of knowing that you were there?" the MacArthur said.

They both nodded.

"That for me was the most interesting part of your story," he said, sitting back in his chair and adjusting some cushions as he fished for his pipe.

"I thought ..." Neil ventured. "I thought that he could smell us. I know it sounds stupid," he added quickly, "but he sort of raised his head and sniffed the air."

There was a deathly silence as Hamish, Jaikie and Arthur stiffened and looked at the MacArthur.

"Does your German teacher have striking blue eyes?" Archie asked in a curious voice.

Neil nodded.

"Pale blue eyes?"

Again Neil nodded and Archie's face turned as white as a sheet.

"The Onegin!" Jaikie whispered, looking at the MacArthur in awe.

"On – yeg – in?" repeated Neil curiously. "Who or what are they?"

"The Wolf People," Hamish breathed, feeling the hairs on the back of his neck rise.

Neil and Clara eyed one another sideways as Arthur sent a streaming curl of fire over the paved floor round the dais. Wolf People?

"I guessed as much," the MacArthur said. "That's why I put a powerful spell on your firestones." He glanced at Neil and Clara. "No one will be able to sense your presence now," he assured them, "neither the witches, nor the wolves. As long as you're wearing your firestones, they won't know you are among them."

"But I don't *want* Neil and Clara to be among

them," Mrs MacLean said jumping to her feet. "The witches were bad enough but wolves as well ..." She turned to her husband, almost in tears. "John, say something!" she implored. "This is dangerous!"

"It does sound dangerous," admitted the Ranger, looking at the MacArthur in some concern. "Who and what are these Wolf People? They sound quite frightening!"

"They *are* frightening," Archie muttered under his breath.

The Wolf People come from the Erevin Mountains in Central Europe, mainly from a little state called Ashgar — where Merial's father lives," the MacArthur said slowly.

"Then, that means that Merial's father, this Lord Jezail, has sent Herr von Grozny to find the talisman!" Neil said in quick understanding.

"From what you've told me about him, I rather think his real name is Count Vassili Onegin," the MacArthur said.

"That figures," Jaikie nodded in agreement and then, seeing their puzzled expressions, added, "he's Lord Jezail's right-hand man."

The MacArthur continued. "You see, I always thought that Lord Jezail would want the talisman back when Merial died. He's too old to search the countryside for it himself so he's sent Count Vassili instead."

"And what if he finds it," the Ranger asked, "or the witches?"

"We need to make sure they don't," the MacArthur said, his face serious. "Merial left the talisman to Clara and it is most important that *she* is the one to find it."

"Yeah," agreed Jaikie, "you've no idea what the witches would get up to if they got hold of it! There would be storms, floods, famine and goodness knows what else. And knowing the Snow Witches — well, personally, I wouldn't put it past them to start another *Ice Age!*"

Mrs MacLean took Clara's hands in hers. "*I* think the talisman should go back to Murial's father ... this Lord Jezail," she urged. "After all, you're not a magic person, Clara."

It was on the tip of Clara's tongue to agree with her mother but to her surprise as much as everyone else's, she found herself shaking her head. "No way, Mum," she answered firmly. "Auntie Muriel wanted *me* to have the talisman and I'm going to find it and use it as she knew I would."

"Well said," the MacArthur smiled and nodded but only Jaikie noticed that his eyes were, nevertheless, doubtful.

"And now," Neil said, having the last word, "all we have to do is find the answer to the riddle!"

12. Snowmen

The car accelerated swiftly as they left Edinburgh and headed south.

"There doesn't seem to be much traffic today, does there?" Neil remarked as his father swung out to overtake a huge trailer. An empty road stretched ahead, winding picturesquely between woods, trees and fields.

"Mmm. If it's like this all the way, we'll have an easy journey," his father replied.

"Perhaps we could stop at Carfrae Mill and have a bite of lunch," Mrs MacLean suggested. "It's roughly halfway to Craiglaw and it'll give you a break from driving, John."

"Great," said Neil, who knew it as a familiar landmark.

"The countryside's changing already, isn't it?" Clara remarked, noticing that the golden fields of waving wheat had disappeared to be replaced by ploughed fields.

"Winter's on its way," her father smiled.

"This is the bit of the journey I like best," Neil said, leaning forward excitedly as they climbed the steep slope towards Soutra Hill and the stretch of moor that held an enormous wind farm. There was a stiff breeze blowing and the blades were swirling fast.

"*I* think they're beautiful," Mrs MacLean said, peering over the moorland at the enormous pylons, "but a lot of people think they spoil the look of the countryside."

It wasn't long after they'd crossed Soutra that the car pulled into the car park of Carfrae Mill. Shivering in the chill wind, they hurried into the welcoming warmth of the hotel lounge and settled by the leaping flames of a log fire. Clara held her hands out to the blaze and when her mother mentioned lentil soup, she nodded her head. It was definitely soup weather!

"It's a lot colder here than it was in Edinburgh," Neil complained, kneeling close to the hearth.

"We don't usually light the fire in the mornings," the waitress said, overhearing him as she laid out the place settings, "but the weather's been that cold lately. They've had snow on the moors above Greenlaw. In October!" she added, shaking her head at the fickleness of the weather.

"We'll be going through Greenlaw," John MacLean looked up from the menu. "The roads are okay, are they?"

"From round about there, are you?" the waitress enquired.

The MacLeans looked at one another. "We're relatively new to the Borders," John MacLean admitted. "We've just moved into a house outside Coldstream."

"Aye, well, just be careful as you go," the waitress cautioned. "There are places where the snow's been awful bad." She seemed to be about to say more but glancing at the two children, just nodded and went away to get their soup.

"She was going to tell you something else, Dad," Neil said, watching her cross the lounge towards the kitchens.

"Yes," Clara agreed. "She didn't want to say anything in front of us."

"I'll have a word with her when I pay the bill," her father said, looking thoughtful. "There must be something odd going on," he lowered his voice, "probably the witches again. The locals in the pub in at Norham were just the same. Looking over their shoulders and whispering in corners."

"And remember that old shepherd we met near Swinton ..." Mrs MacLean added. "He believed in witches all right."

"They're close to the earth, the shepherds," her husband nodded seriously, "and they know when nature's out of kilter."

"Well, Dad," Neil asked as the car swung out onto the main road again, "what did she say?"

"Nothing specific," his father answered. "Apparently there's been a lot of snow and the farmers have had to bring their sheep in from the fields."

"There isn't much up there on the moors," Mrs MacLean frowned, "apart from a few odd farms. Muriel took me to visit some friends of hers who live up there. What were their names again?" she frowned, trying to remember. "Nice people. We had tea with them."

The road started to climb through the fields and as they passed farm after farm, the weather became positively icy. "Look, the snow's starting," Clara said as white flakes swirled around the car.

"Have you got the heater on full, John?" Mrs MacLean asked and as he nodded she shivered and drew her coat tighter. "It certainly doesn't feel like it!" she grumbled.

"Let me concentrate on the driving, Janet," he said irritably, peering forward through the windscreen as huge snowflakes slid down the glass. "The snow's getting worse."

"Thank goodness we've got a 4x4," Neil said thankfully. "They can take pretty much anything."

There was silence in the car as the snow grew heavier. They were now on the long road that ran across the moors and as the snow thickened to a blizzard, John MacLean reduced his speed to a crawl. A line of pine trees stretched in a straight line to their right and further on, to their left, a glint of light shone from a farmhouse window. Bent forward over the wheel, he concentrated on a road that had, by this time, almost disappeared altogether. As long as he didn't land in a ditch, that was the main thing, he reckoned.

"There's a farm coming up, John," his wife said, rubbing her breath from the car window so that she could see through. "Aren't you going to stop?"

"I can see people outside in the snow," Clara said excitedly. "They're all dressed in white." She frowned. "That's a bit odd, isn't it?"

Her father looked undecided for a moment. "Maybe I *should* stop and pull into the farm," he said, braking carefully and putting the car into reverse. "I'm sure the farmer would look after us until the storm passes. Blast! I can't even see the turning."

"Do you want me to get out, Dad?" Neil asked.

"No, stay where you are just now, Neil," his father said, opening the car door and climbing out. "I just want to see if we've passed the farm road."

"Can you see any witches?" Mrs MacLean peered through the open door.

"Not one," he said, scanning the sky through the swirling flakes. "Maybe this *is* just freak weather. Everyone's talking about climate change these days ..."

Mrs MacLean turned white all of a sudden and pointed dramatically at the sky behind him. Seeing her look of fear, her husband swung round and stared at the ragged tops of the massive stand of pine trees that lined the road. "Witches! They're there, John! Hiding among the trees! Look!"

"Mum's right, Dad," Clara yelled, winding her window down to get a clearer view. She pointed as the blizzard eased momentarily. "They're there! Over to your ... right ..." She gulped and her voice faded as the Queen of the Snow Witches swooped out of the trees towards the car, her witches outlined behind her against a leaden sky.

Samantha recognized Clara immediately. Surely this was the child she'd kidnapped in Argyle a few years back at the request of Prince Kalman. The child who'd somehow managed to escape her clutches! She boiled with rage at the thought, for the prince had been really most unpleasant when he heard she'd been rescued. Samantha smiled malevolently. This was her chance to punish her!

She'd bury her under six feet of snow if she had to! "Get them," she shrieked as she wheeled towards the staring occupants of the car.

"Get in quick, John," Mrs MacLean said urgently.

"Put your window up, Clara," John MacLean said, slipping into the driver's seat and turning the key in the ignition as the witches dive-bombed the 4x4 with inches to spare.

The car started but the engine was rough and, at first, it lurched forward in a series of jerks before moving more smoothly. John peered through the swishing windscreen wipers trying to gauge where the edge of the road was.

"There's a car ahead of us," Mrs MacLean said suddenly, peering through a sudden break in the storm. "It's miles ahead but I'm sure I saw its rear lights through the snow!"

"Dad!" Clara yelled. Her father slammed on the brakes and they all fell forwards against their seat belts.

"What is it?" her father asked, twisting round in his seat.

Clara pointed through the window. "The men on the farm," she gasped, "they're not people at all. Look at them! Can't you see their faces? They're snowmen!" she whispered. "Look! Look, over there! They're heading for the road!"

Neil gasped. Clara was right. Running towards the car with lumbering steps were several white, bulky figures. Snowmen! Snowmen with carrot noses and black stone eyes! "Come on, Dad! Put your foot down," Neil yelled, "they're catching up with us." As the car pulled away, the snowmen halted but they hadn't finished. Bending down they lifted handfuls of snow and Clara cringed as the first volley of snowballs crashed against the rear window.

"For goodness sake, keep going, John," Mrs MacLean urged. "We've got to catch up with that car in front."

The witches, however, were determined to stop them. The snow became heavier and as more and more snowmen rose from the side of the road, John sent it skating and slithering in as straight a line as he could manage. Although the snowballs did no real damage, the melting snowflakes, sliding down the windscreen, reduced visibility to little more than a few feet. It was really scary, Clara admitted afterwards, for the other windows were so snowed up on the outside that they didn't know whether the snowmen were running alongside them or not.

It was when one of them threw itself in front of the 4x4 that John MacLean gunned the engine and bounced the car over it with a bump that would have sent them all through the windscreen had they not had their seat belts on.

"There it is, John," Mrs MacLean said in triumph as two red lights shone in front of them, "I told you there was a car in front of us."

"He's seen our lights," Neil said. "Look, he's blinking his hazard lights at us."

John MacLean breathed a sigh of relief. "He's waiting for us to catch up with him."

This didn't stop the snowmen, however, and both cars came under fire from volleys of snowballs that hit the cars with dull, heavy thumps. It was only when they reached the first houses in Greenlaw that the snowmen faded from the scene and by the time they drew up in front of the general store they were weak with relief.

The driver of the other car pulled up in front of them and came over; a pleasant, dark-haired chap with blue eyes. John MacLean smiled at him. "Thank goodness you were on the road! If we hadn't had you to follow we might never have made it through!"

"It was quite an experience, wasn't it? And the hailstones! I've never see anything like the size of them in my life!" He looked up the road. "They need to get the snowplough up there, pronto," he continued without waiting for an answer. "I've not seen weather as bad as this in a long time!"

Neil and Clara looked at one another with raised eyebrows. He probably never would again, Neil thought. But hailstones! How *could* he think that! They'd been thumping great snowballs!

13. Bad news

Kitor fluttered his wings anxiously as the car turned into the driveway of Craiglaw House.

"Hi, Kitor," Neil said with a smile as the crow landed on his shoulder as he got out of the car. "You found your way alright, then!"

"We got here ages ago!" Kitor said, digging his claws into Neil's jacket to keep his balance "We thought you'd ... got lost or something."

"What kept you?" Cassia asked anxiously, perching on Clara's arm. "We were just going out to look for you."

"We almost *did* have an accident," Mrs MacLean said grimly, pulling a carrier bag out of the car and heading for the front door. "The Snow Witches were out in force on the road near Greenlaw."

"They did their best to stop us," Neil added, "but we managed to keep going."

Kitor squawked. "What happened?"

"The Queen of the Snow Witches recognized me, Kitor," Clara said. "It was really scary. They were using snowmen to search the farm buildings and they attacked us."

Kitor paled at the mention of the Snow Witches. He knew they hadn't forgiven him for rescuing Clara.

"Actually, we didn't cross the moors," Cassia confessed.

Clara, now in safe surroundings, forgot her fear of the Snow Witches and grinned. "I know," she said, looking at Neil in amusement, "you came as the crow flies."

Seeing Kitor's puzzled look, Neil explained. "It's a saying we have in English. It means you didn't follow the roads, you flew in a straight line."

Cassia tilted her head to one side. "It's the only way to fly," she pointed out reasonably. "Why should we follow the roads?"

"Forget it!" Neil said dryly, "or we'll be here all night!"

"No you won't," his mother said, overhearing their conversation. "Go and get your stuff together and put it in the car. We've to get you back to school this evening, remember?"

"Oh no," Neil groaned, "and I haven't even *looked* at my German grammar! Von Grozny's given us a string of verbs to learn!"

"What about the broomsticks?" John MacLean asked. "You're going to look a bit odd going into school with a couple of broomsticks, aren't you?"

"Oh, that's all right," Clara said airily, "I'll say they're for the school play. It's about witches. Nobody'll think anything of it."

"Get yourselves organized then," their mother said briskly, "while I make the supper and defrost some chicken livers for Kitor and Cassia. If they're going on a witch hunt, they'll need all the energy they can get."

As it happened, it didn't take Kitor and Cassia long to suss out the witches.

The following morning, the two crows had swooped from Clara's window not only to take stock of their new surroundings but to search the Border roads for their breakfast. Kitor's eyes had glistened happily, for the good news was that fast food in the shape of squashed rabbit and hedgehog had proved unexpectedly plentiful — and pheasant an unexpected treat. The bad news, however, was that there were witches absolutely everywhere.

Later that evening, Neil looked at his watch and opened his window. It was eight o'clock, the time they'd agreed upon to get together. He shivered in the sudden blast of cold air that whistled through the window and sighed with relief as Kitor and Cassia flew in followed by an invisible Clara who swished past him on her broomstick. Closing the window quickly, he drew the curtains again and turned on the light as Clara switched her ring to her other hand and appeared. Kitor and Cassia perched on the back of a chair, settling their wings as she propped her broomstick against Neil's wardrobe door.

"Hi, Neil," she smiled, "no visitors this evening?"

"Not with all the German verbs I've to swot up," her brother admitted. He turned to the crow. "Well, Kitor?" he queried. "How did you get on today? Find anything out?"

"There are witches everywhere," Kitor announced importantly, fluttering over to Neil's desk and pacing its length in stiff, strutting steps. He looked at them through black, sparkling eyes.

"It's a massive operation they've mounted. Every field, every wood, every farm ... they're going over them all."

"We know all about that," nodded Clara, warming herself against a radiator. "They haven't half given the locals the heeby-jeebies!"

"We spotted your witch on her way back to the school as well," Cassia croaked. "She came from a place called Witches' Wood."

Neil looked up interestedly. He'd heard the name before and then remembered that it had been on the night he'd seen the crop circles being made.

"Witches' Wood is well named," Kitor said. "It covers the top of a steep hill quite near here. That's where the Earth Witches have their castle — inside the hill."

"A castle," Neil's eyebrows shot up, "inside a hill? Then ... that means their castle must be on Blackriggs Farm!" Clara looked blank. "You know ... Jimmy MacFarlane's farm ... where the crop circles keep appearing!" He turned to Kitor. "How on earth did you find it?"

"It wasn't hard to spot," Kitor said dryly. "Busy as a wasps' nest, it was; witches flying in and out all the time. We couldn't go in, of course, for they had witches guarding the entrance."

"But we got close enough to see what it looks like," Cassia added. "There are long, stone passages that go deep inside the hill."

"We hung around for a while and listened to the witches talking," Kitor continued. "They mentioned the talisman so our ears pricked up, as you can imagine. They're over the moon about it."

"About what?" queried Clara, anxiously. "They haven't found it, have they?"

Kitor shook his head. "No, but the Queen of the Earth Witches discovered an ancient book in their library. They called it *The Book of Spells*. From the way they were talking, I reckon it must have been lost for centuries."

"And?" demanded Neil.

"And it's bad news," croaked Cassia. "There's a spell in it that will draw the talisman to her ..."

"... from wherever it is!" finished Kitor.

Clara looked every bit as appalled as Neil. A magic spell that would find the talisman! The witches had to be stopped!

14. Witches' Wood

A few days later, Clara sat on the edge of Neil's bed, catching her hair in a twist on top of her head so that it wouldn't blow all over her face while she was flying on her broomstick.

"Are you both ready?" Kitor asked, fluttering from the back of a chair onto the window sill. "Cassia's keeping watch outside, just in case."

Neil and Clara had never quite managed to understand how they heard Kitor speak. He wasn't, of course, speaking English as such but they could hear his voice inside their heads; although, as Clara remarked, the sound didn't seem to come through their ears.

Neil picked up his broomstick and nodded. "You go first, Clara," he said, disappearing from view as he switched his ring to the other hand.

Kitor soared out over the window sill into space and, grasping her broomstick tightly, Clara followed. She'd always hated heights but flying from the tower window was a piece of cake compared to some of the mountains she'd flown over in the past. Once they reached the level of the trees, however, she felt a lot more comfortable and started to take an interest in her surroundings. Cassia, she noticed, had flown up to join Kitor and

the two broomsticks settled in behind them as they
headed over the school grounds for Witches' Wood.

"Leave your broomsticks here," Kitor whispered
as they dismounted at the edge of a newly-ploughed
field. "Cassia and I will look after them for you."

"Is that the hill, over there?" Neil hissed,
looking at the grassy, rounded hill topped by a
stand of trees that rose steeply from the swirling
pattern of furrows that surrounded it.

Kitor nodded. "You'll see the entrance on the
right," he whispered. "It's quite wide; so that the
broomsticks can get in and out, I suppose. Just
be careful you don't bump into anybody. They
mightn't be able to see you but if they touch you,
they'll know you're there."

Neil nodded. "We'll be careful," he whispered as
they made to leave, "don't worry!"

He and Clara picked their invisible way carefully
over the newly-turned furrows towards the
entrance to the witches' lair. Without her firestone,
Clara thought, she'd probably have seen a normal,
peaceful country scene but wearing it changed
everything. There were witches everywhere. Some
were soaring over distant woods and fields but it
was quite obvious where the entrance to the castle
lay, for witches were coming and going all the time.
It was breath-taking to watch as, crouched low
over the handles of their broomsticks, they flew
past them in the moonlight, their cloaks fluttering
and flapping behind them as they swooped through
the night sky.

Neil gulped at the sight of their evil, intent
faces, suddenly aware of the dangers they were

facing. Just as well, he thought, that their parents didn't know what they were up to! "Keep hold of my hand, Clara," he whispered, trying to sound reassuring, "and remember what I said; if you lose me, get out at once and go back to Kitor and Cassia, okay?"

"Okay," Clara said, her voice trembling with fear and excitement.

Neil's hand tightened its grip as they reached the damp stonework of the entrance. The flat, grey slabs of stone that sloped steeply downwards were running with moisture and here and there bushes and clumps of creeping fern straggled in swathes over their cracked, uneven sides. Crouching down to avoid the broomsticks that were flying in and out over their heads, they paused and eyed the witches on guard apprehensively. Perched like ragged crows atop thin, spindly rocks round the entrance, they were screeching and cackling to one another but gave no sign of alarm as, choosing a moment when no broomsticks were in sight, they slipped silently down the passage into the hill.

The interior of the Earth Witches' castle was astounding. Built from huge blocks of pale grey stone it was a vast construction. Carved arches revealed long, eerie passageways decorated here and there with statues of wizards, witches and other magical creatures that looked so ghastly that Clara hoped fervently that she'd never have to meet them.

Neither was it as dark as they had expected, but full of a ghostly white light that threw deep shadows.

Choosing the broadest of the three corridors that confronted them so that there was less likelihood of bumping into anyone, they walked silently along, hugging the wall. At first, all went well. Several witches flew past them on broomsticks but as they paid them no attention whatsoever Clara relaxed and had almost persuaded herself that everything was going to be okay when a chattering group of young witches approached. Cloaks flapping, they took up the whole width of the corridor so that they both had to press themselves flat against the wall. Clara felt her heart thump alarmingly as the witches brushed past, their strong, hook-nosed faces so close that she could have reached out and touched them. She was shaking violently as she felt for Neil's hand and gripped it hard.

After that, they passed several groups of witches, many of them talking and laughing in the same high-pitched cackle of sound they'd heard from the witches on guard at the entrance. These witches, however, were easily avoided as they kept to the centre of the corridor and, glad that there was no repeat of the first nerve-racking incident, they walked on with steadily increasing confidence until they came to a flight of stairs that led deeper into the earth. Clara wasn't all that keen on going down but Neil pulled on her hand and she had to follow.

They moved further and further through the maze of corridors, peering into all the rooms, until they came at last to a door of obvious importance. A heavy, black, iron-studded door, which swung open as they approached.

Clara stopped dead in her tracks. She couldn't believe her eyes and almost fell over at the shock of it, for there, as large as life, walking in the middle of a group of witches, was her Drama teacher. It must have been Miss Markham she'd seen at school that night!

How had she not realized that she was a witch? All the signs were there: the hooked nose, the strong features, the black hair and piercing eyes. How on *earth* hadn't she noticed?

It was then that Neil jerked her to one side as the witches passed in a swirl of black robes. Miss Markham was frowning and talking sharply to a thin, seedy-looking witch whose robes shed lumps of earth as she walked.

"It'll come to me eventually," she was saying. "I said the spell several times and each time I felt it trying to obey."

Clara barely heard her words. She was still in shock! Miss Markham was a witch! Neil pulled her hastily forward and caught the door before it closed. He'd glimpsed what lay beyond it as the witches had swung through and his heart had leapt. This was what they were looking for; the witches' library.

The heavy door clicked shut behind them and left them standing in a totally silent room that almost literally took their breath away. It smelled incredibly ancient and they knew instinctively that the room and its contents were thousands of years old.

And what books! Thick, heavy volumes with ragged, irregular pages made from parchment, not paper — the room was crammed with them. They lay on shelves, on tables and in scattered piles all over the floor. Books of all shapes and sizes, thousands of them, bound in old, rubbed leather that looked as though a touch would crumble them to dust.

Creeping quietly round tiers of shelving, they found, to their horror, that the library wasn't empty as they had first thought. Two witches were sitting at a corner table, reading from an enormous tome and making copious notes while another browsed through smaller volumes in a bookcase nearby.

What caught their eyes immediately, however, was a huge table, set to one side in a position of importance. It held only one book, a large volume that lay open on a carved book rest and it was interest, more than anything else that drew Neil towards it. They both froze, however, as they saw the detailed drawing that decorated the top of the right-hand page. An arm clasp, the MacArthur had said. A silver arm clasp. Clara knew immediately that it was the talisman. Neil squeezed her hand to tell her that he, too, recognized the description. This must be the book that contained the talisman spell — the book that Miss Markham had found.

The words on the page were meaningless, written in an unknown language, but as Clara's eyes read them avidly, they printed themselves on her brain and she knew, beyond a shadow of doubt, that this was the book they'd come for. Impulsively, she reached out her hands and drew the heavy covers closed to take it. It was a very old book, however, and didn't close easily. Its ancient covers creaked alarmingly and the pages made a rough whisper of sound as she stuffed it under her coat.

Neil stiffened and glanced at the witches. One of them looked up at the sudden noise and scanned the room curiously, but seeing no one, returned to her task. He held his breath. Had she really seen nothing? He couldn't be sure.

Nerves made him grab Clara's arm hard but she barely noticed. Now that she had *The Book of Spells* firmly clasped to her chest, she was just as anxious as he was to get away. Moving steadily towards the door, Neil hoped fervently that the witches wouldn't notice that the book had disappeared. The empty book rest would tell its own story: there was no doubt about it; it would soon be missed.

They met their first setback when they reached the door. Neil couldn't open it. He heaved at the ringed handle with all his strength but it was no good. Clara clutched at his arm. How, she thought, were they going to get out?

Neil put his mouth to where he roughly thought Clara's ear must be. "Calm down," he whispered in a voice that was barely a breath. "It'll be okay. We'll just have to wait until somebody comes in."

Clara bit her lip with frustration. She clutched the book tighter and prayed that the witches wouldn't notice it was gone. What if one of the witches needed to consult the book and found that it had disappeared? The alarm would be raised and they'd be trapped. The very idea left her feeling positively weak at the knees. She stared at the heavy iron hinges and round studs that decorated the door and desperately willed it to open.

In actual fact, barely ten minutes passed before the door swung inwards but it felt more like ten hours to Neil and Clara. The witches that entered were carrying notebooks. More students, Neil thought thankfully as he caught the door as it started to swing to and pushed Clara through ahead of him.

Witches filled the corridors outside and although Neil had the sense to move carefully, his every instinct was to run madly for the safety of the field. Calm down, he told himself sternly, or you'll make mistakes and be caught. Keeping well to the side of the corridor, they came to the flight of shallow stairs that led upwards. Once at the top, they wouldn't really have far to go, he thought, and as long as no one bumped into them, they should be safe enough.

Clara, meanwhile, was in a fever of excitement. They'd got the book and now all they had to do was walk out of this dreadful place. Thank goodness, she thought, that the MacArthur had put extra magic into their firestones. The witches would surely have sensed their presence otherwise and that would have been a disaster.

By the time they reached the long, wide corridor that led to the entrance, their spirits were starting to rise and just when Neil thought they'd got away with it, they heard the distant, screeching screams of the witches. Clara's heart sank. The book had been missed!

The old hags, perched like vultures on their rocky perches over the entrance, stopped their cackling and alerted by a hullabaloo that was getting louder by the second, sat up and took notice. Neil turned and saw witches pouring in a sweeping tide behind them and, throwing caution to the winds, urged Clara on at a run. What really worried him was the thought that the witches might close the entrance with a hex. And there wasn't a lot they could do if *that* happened ...

The old hags, now awake to the threat of danger, were slithering like evil spiders from their perches and almost landed on top of them. They were seconds too late, however, for even as they dropped on all fours to the ground, blocking the entrance, Neil and Clara were through and already scrambling up the steep little slope that gave onto the field.

It was only when he felt the soft earth under his feet that Neil let his breath out in a long sigh of relief. They'd done it! They'd got away with *The Book of Spells*. He pulled triumphantly on Clara's hand and, with that, they both started to run pell-mell across the furrows.

"Kitor! Cassia! We're here!" Neil hissed as they reached the edge of the field. Looking round, they found their broomsticks where they'd left them, lying lengthwise in the shadow of the old stone wall that bounded the field.

Kitor breathed a sigh of relief as he heard Neil's voice. The hue and cry that had erupted from the entrance to the witches' castle had told him that they had been discovered and his heart had been in his mouth as he'd looked across the field, hoping against hope that they'd escaped.

"Hurry," he urged, flapping down to perch on the stone wall, "the witches will be here any minute!"

"Got your broomstick, Clara?" Neil whispered as he saw it lift off the ground and disappear.

"Yes," she whispered. "Come on, Neil! For goodness sake, let's get out of here!"

Kitor and Cassia flapped heavily into the night air and as his broomstick soared skywards, Neil took one last look across the field and grinned, despite himself, at the total confusion that reigned round the little hill. Witches were soaring and swooping round the tree-tops like so many bats.

Even as the crows flapped off, however, an old man emerged silently from among the trees. Walking up to the stone wall as the crows disappeared from sight over a nearby wood, he turned and looked speculatively across the field where two lines of footprints showed clearly in the moonlight. A sour smile curved his lips. Neil and Clara still had a lot to learn. The witches were a sharp lot and not easy to fool. He lifted his hand and as he murmured the words of a hex, the footprints in the field blurred and vanished.

15. Drama queen

"I'm sorry, Maritza," the Deputy Head said, looking somewhat stunned as he regarded the massive castle from his vantage point in the wings, "it's a truly wonderful set, but you really *should* have consulted me before you put it up, you know."

"Perhaps you could tell me *exactly* what's wrong with it?" the Drama teacher said, her hackles rising almost visibly as she strode onto the stage. "*Look at it*," she waved her arms around in a gesture that embraced the entire castle — turrets, battlements and all. "Just *look* at it! It's a fantastic set! *Everybody* says so!"

"It's not suitable, that's all," he answered.

Maritza regarded him coldly. This, she thought furiously, was all she needed! That she'd had a bad night was putting things mildly. Deeply worried at the loss of *The Book of Spells* and unsure as to which of the witches had managed to steal it, she was in no mood to be trifled with. Her eyes narrowed angrily. The Deputy's criticism of her beautiful set did nothing to improve her temper; indeed, she looked as though she were about to erupt. "What do you want me to do with it then?" she snapped. "Take it all down?"

Sensing danger, the Deputy Head backed off at the threat of a confrontation. The trouble with all the Drama teachers he'd ever met, he thought sourly, was their in-built tendency to go totally over the top at the drop of a hat. He looked again round the stage where the turrets of the huge castle loomed stark and clear against a stormy sky, the yellow glow of the full moon half hidden by clouds. He pursed his lips undecidedly. There was no getting away from it, he thought, it was a fantastic set. Possibly the best he'd ever seen for a school concert.

"It would break my heart to have to take it all down," Maritza pleaded, changing her approach — whilst wondering if she shouldn't just hex him into agreeing to it there and then.

"Well ..." he frowned.

"We put so much work into it," she added, laying on the pathos with a trowel.

"Look, most of it's fine," he agreed, trying to sound encouraging. "It's the battlements that are the problem." He pointed to a staircase that curved upwards to a broad platform that was backed by a length of crenellated stonework. "That platform affair is quite a height, you know. Do you really need it?"

The Queen of the Witches took a deep breath and held on to her temper with an effort. "Of course I need it," she said in a voice only slightly tinged with exasperation. "It's used all the time! A whole chorus of witches stands up there in Act II. It's ... it's the most dramatic part of the play!"

"In that case, it'll almost certainly have to come

down," the Deputy Head said stiffly. "We can't risk having any of the children falling off. I mean, one of them might forget and just step backwards. The crenellations at the back aren't high enough to stop anyone going over and the stage," he said crisply, "is a long way down."

Just then, the History master walked onto the stage and whistled appreciatively as he looked round. "Some set, Maritza," he nodded.

Maritza eyed the Deputy sideways and accepted the praise gratefully. "Thank you, Ross," she said, inclining her head graciously. "I'm glad *somebody* likes it!"

"I'm not saying it's not a good set," muttered the Deputy. "Actually, I think it's fabulous but I *am* Health and Safety officer for the school and we just can't have a whole load of children prancing up and down on those battlements with nothing behind them. You know how excited they get during shows ... ten to one someone would do a bit of pushing and shoving and bingo — a nightmare situation for the school!"

"He wants me to take the whole thing down, Ross," she said angrily as the History master prowled the stage.

"Oh, I shouldn't think there's any need for that," came the answer as Ross walked through an archway and peered round the back of the set. "I'd have said the solution was pretty obvious, really!"

"What?" Maritza's head jerked in surprise.

"Come and have a look," Ross Wilson invited and, as they stepped behind the castle, he pointed to the space below the battlements. "All you need is a couple of mattresses," he said, "and then, if anybody does fall off, there'll be no harm done."

"You're a genius, Ross," Maritza clapped her hands.

"You're right," the Deputy Head sighed with relief, "and no need for proper mattresses, either. You can use the mats from the gym."

"I will arrange it," Maritza said, her black eyes flashing in relief. "Now gentlemen," she looked at her watch, "I have a rehearsal in five minutes and still many things to do. The mats first of all!"

"The funniest bit of the rehearsal," Clara confided to Neil later when she flew over to his room, "was when Angela fooled around with the cauldron and Sandra stuffed a plastic spider down her blazer."

"Is that all?" Neil looked up in surprise as he finished sorting out his homework. "*I* heard there was a bit of a stink about the set?"

"Really?" Clara said, interestedly. "We never heard anything about *that*."

"Well, we had History after break and Mr Wilson told us that the Deputy Head was threatening to have it all pulled down!"

"Pulled down!" Clara echoed, looking horrified. "*No way!*"

Neil raised his eyebrows. "Good, is it?"

"Haven't you *seen* it yet?" she asked in surprise and as he shook his head, added. "It's the most fabulous set I've ever seen; a really super castle. Dead creepy."

"I bet she hexed it up in a couple of seconds," Neil

replied, only half listening as, for the hundredth time, he took out his copy of the riddle and stared at it as though hoping the answer would jump out at him.

"I almost forget to tell you," Clara continued. "We tested one of the harnesses. Monica put on hers and flew from one side of the wings to the other on a broomstick. It'll look great on the night but she looked a bit stupid in school uniform. Everyone cheered and Miss Markham was furious. I thought she was going to hex us all! I'm not surprised that everybody hates her; she was in *such* a foul mood today!"

"I'm not surprised, after last night," grinned Neil. "She must be worried out of her mind." He looked at her anxiously. "Where did you put *The Book of Spells,* by the way?"

"I've hidden it on top of my wardrobe under some school books," Clara admitted. "I hope it's safe. If the witches find out that it was us that took it ..." she shivered at the thought.

"The MacArthur's spell protected us," Neil pointed out reasonably. "You know that! The witches didn't sense that anyone else was around at all."

"You never know, we might have left a clue behind that'll bring them straight here."

"Give over, Clara," Neil looked irritated. "You're worrying about nothing."

"I can't help it, Neil," Clara admitted. "I'm really scared of Miss Markham. Maybe we should ask Kitor and Cassia to go to Arthur's Seat and tell the MacArthur what we've been up to and ... and ask about *The Book of Spells,* as well. What do you think?"

Neil frowned. "Where *is* Kitor?" he asked.

"They're both in my room, perched on the chair beside the radiator," Clara answered with a reluctant smile. "Either my room's much more comfortable for roosting in than the trees or they're guarding *The Book of Spells!*"

"You could take the book home and hide it there," Neil suggested, looking at his watch. "It would take you about an hour to get to Craiglaw and back on your broomstick. What about it?"

Clara shook her head. "That's not a good idea, Neil. I'd rather send Kitor and Cassia back to the hill for if the witches suspect anyone of stealing *The Book of Spells,* it'll be either the Wind Witches or the Snow Witches. I reckon they'll be on the look-out for broomsticks ... any broomsticks!"

"You're right," Neil agreed, "I didn't think of that." He looked at her anxious face and smiled. "Calm down," he said. "We'll send Kitor and Cassia off tonight. Okay?"

"Great," Clara said, relief colouring her voice. "That makes me feel a lot better."

Neil nodded. "It's just as well we don't need the broomsticks at the moment — apart from flying between our rooms, that is." He grinned mischievously. "Face it, Clara! You'll just have to make do with the harness in the school play for now!"

Clara shook her head. "Actually, I don't get to fly at all," she grinned. "I'm one of the "pretend" witches."

Neil looked at her sideways. "What on earth's a 'pretend' witch?"

"Well," Clara shrugged, "some of us are kids playing at being witches and the others are supposed to be 'real' witches."

"So you're not one of the stars!" Neil teased.

"I don't want to be," she assured him. "Not with Miss Markham around."

"Yeah," Neil nodded, "I'll keep out of her way, too, just in case she senses any magic in me."

"The play's quite good fun otherwise, though," Clara continued. "I got to know one or two of the girls better this morning. Angela seems really nice and on the days her dad's late in picking her up, I've asked her to come to my room."

"Good," Neil looked across at her and was relieved to see that she looked more like her old self. It had worried him that Clara seemed to be on her own all the time once classes finished. "Why's the play called *Pumpkin Pie*, by the way? It seems to be all about witches."

"We find a spell in an old book and change our pumpkin into a magic one that conjures up bats and owls and real witches. We all run away and the real witches change it into a pie."

"Doesn't sound very exciting," Neil grumbled.

"I know — it sounds nothing the way I'm telling it, but it's actually quite good," Clara grinned. "Anyway, cheer up! Miss Markham's got the kitchen staff organized and you're all going to get a huge slice of pumpkin pie at the end of the dress rehearsal."

Neil's eyes brightened. "Mightn't be so bad, then!"

Clara looked at her watch and sighed. Time to be getting back, she thought. She still had some homework to finish as well. She looked at Neil somewhat guiltily. It wasn't that she wanted to hide anything from him but somehow she just couldn't tell him how *The Book of Spells* fascinated her. The dusty pages of old parchment, the funny old-fashioned writing and strange magic words that she couldn't understand seemed to send her into a dream and although she wouldn't admit it, even to herself, she knew perfectly well that the spells that she read were imprinted in her memory. "Did you have any luck with Mrs Weston?" she asked, seeing the riddle lying beside his Maths book.

Neil shook his head. "No, I didn't have a chance," he admitted. "The Geography teacher's off sick and she's taking some of his classes. I'll try and see her tomorrow."

"Do you really think she might work it out for us?" Clara asked, taking her magic ring off.

"Well, she was Auntie Muriel's friend and Mum said they always did the *Scotsman* crossword together at break."

"You'll have to ask her not to mention it to anyone," Clara warned, slipping the ring onto her left hand and disappearing entirely as she reached for her broomstick.

Neil nodded as he turned to open the window for her. "I won't forget," he said.

16. Riddle-me-ree

"Of course, I'd be delighted to help you, Neil," Mrs Weston said with a smile, scanning the riddle thoughtfully as the rest of his class drifted out at the end of the lesson. "It's strange that Muriel said nothing to me about riddles but it certainly looks intriguing."

"My mother said you were good at puzzles," Neil said, "so we're hoping you might be able to solve it for us."

"In that case, I suggest that you keep the original sheet, Neil, and give me a copy. Just in case I lose it! Here," she said, reaching for a sheet of paper, "why don't you take this and copy it down for me."

"Thanks, Mrs Weston," he said gratefully, moving towards one of the desks, "it won't take a minute."

He picked up a pencil and wrote:

The Talisman

Beside the firelight
Lies your treasure
A talisman from ages past
Cast in silver, steeped in magic
Keep it safe and use it well

> Bind it to you, meet its challenge
> Until it's time to pass it on
> Look to Morven's Lords for guidance
> Let their wisdom rule your choice

"That's it finished," he said, getting up and handing her the paper as the classroom started to fill with sixth formers.

"Right, that's fine," she said, glancing at it briefly before folding the sheet in half and slipping it inside a book of poems. "I'm afraid it'll be break before I have a chance to look at it," she apologized. "As you see, I have a class now."

Although Neil tried to hide his disappointment, his face fell noticeably.

"Don't worry," she assured him. "I'll catch up with you later on in the day. Promise!"

"I've got rugby practice after lunch," Neil said, suddenly wishing that all his classes had been in the main building that afternoon.

"I'll find you," she said, seeing his worried look.

"And you won't tell anyone, will you?" he whispered. "It's a secret ..."

"My lips are sealed," she assured him seriously. And her eyes were kind.

Herr von Grozny raised his eyebrows as Neil knocked on the door and entered the classroom with a muttered apology.

"Where were you, Neil, to be so late?" he queried in German. "The rest of the class managed to arrive in good time."

"I was with ..."

"In German, please!" Von Grozny's tone was haughty.

Neil took a deep breath and marshalled his thoughts. "I had a question to ask Mrs Weston and it took longer than I thought." He looked doubtfully at von Grozny, almost sure that he'd made a horrendous mistake with his endings somewhere along the line. The icy blue eyes should have frozen him solid but, for an instant, he thought he caught more than a flicker of amusement in his glance.

"Very well, Neil. Sit down and get your book out. We are on page 175, the perfect tense."

Neil slipped into his seat and made a face at George as he rummaged through his bag for his German grammar. It wasn't there. His heart sank. He'd left it in his room, hadn't he? Blast, it had probably slipped down the side of his bed and he just hadn't noticed.

"We are waiting for you, Neil ..." von Grozny's was smooth and unhurried, almost as if he knew the book wasn't there.

"Sir, I ..." Neil rummaged some more.

"In German, please."

"I'm very sorry, Herr von Grozny, but I was ..." he gulped, "I was learning my verbs in bed last night and I think I must have fallen asleep and ... and ..."

Von Grozny sighed. "Are you trying to tell me that your German grammar book is in your bed?" he said gravely.

Neil nodded, his face red with embarrassment. The class, however, seeing von Grozny's lips twitch in amusement, burst out laughing.

"Since you have already wasted so much time, I suggest you share George's book," von Grozny said as the laughter died away, "but first we'll see how much you remember, shall we?"

Neil eyed him apprehensively. He wasn't really worried as he'd been studying hard. The man demanded high standards and Neil felt he would rather die than fall short of them. Indeed, he was beginning to have serious doubts at his assertion that von Grozny was using magic to teach him.

"Now, Neil," von Grozny began. The questioning went on for some time until some of the class shifted uncomfortably, feeling that the inquisition had gone on long enough. Von Grozny took no notice and by the time he had finished, Neil felt totally washed out. Nevertheless, he'd only made two mistakes and felt that he hadn't done at all badly.

"So," von Grozny nodded thoughtfully, 'very well done, Neil. You look like becoming our star pupil. Didn't you tell me that you hadn't studied German before you came to the school?"

"I did French in Edinburgh, Sir," Neil answered readily enough.

"You obviously have a flair for languages, Neil. Three house points."

There was a gasp from the rest of the class. To get one house point out of the German master was an achievement. Three was unheard of.

The rest of lesson proceeded as normal and it was as they filed out that George whispered. "You did really well out of that!"

Neil flushed and was about to answer angrily when George looked at his face and put a hand on his arm. "Don't be daft," he said. "I'm not talking about the house points. You deserved them. It's just that if anyone else had forgotten their German grammar he'd have really blasted them, you know he would!"

"Maybe he knows that I like the language," Neil said doubtfully. "I don't know what it is about German, I just like it. More than I did French."

"I wish *I* did," George answered enviously. "I'm useless. I always forget to put the verb at the end of the sentence."

Herr von Grozny sat back in his chair as the class filed out and tapped a pencil thoughtfully on the wood of his desk. He knew perfectly well that it had been Neil and Clara that he'd nearly caught in the library. He'd picked up their scent immediately and wondered idly if they knew he'd guessed their identity. Lady Merial's niece and nephew. That had been a real eye-opener. He'd picked up the gossip in the staff room almost by accident.

Should he patrol the corridors again that night? He pursed his lips and sighed inwardly for so far his searches of the school and the surrounding countryside had yielded nothing and his master, too, was becoming steadily more and more irritated at his lack of progress. Indeed, the increasingly angry exchanges through the crystal made him wish that he'd never mentioned the two children for, although he'd kept a wary eye on the staircases that led to the towers, neither of them had ventured out in the dark to explore the school since. He'd have picked up their scent otherwise. And Neil had, indeed, been telling the truth when he'd said he'd spent the night learning his verbs. He sighed. Maybe he was attaching too much importance to them but the fact remained that they both wore magic rings and must, like the witches, be looking for the talisman.

He saw her coming towards him as he left the Rugby pitch, totally knackered, spattered with mud but over the moon, nevertheless, as he'd scored a try.

"Great game, Neil!"

"Well done, Neil!"

He grinned and waved his thanks as his mates who, seeing Mrs Weston approach with the obvious intention of collaring him, sloped off towards the changing rooms.

Neil's heart jumped as he saw that Mrs Weston, clutching her coat to her in the biting wind, had a beaming smile on her face. She's solved it, he thought. By golly, she's solved it!

"You know the answer, don't you," he said eagerly, running towards her.

"Yes, I do," she laughed. "It was very easy really!"

"Easy!" Neil said. "Clara and I *and* my mum and dad have been trying to work it out for weeks now!"

"You should have brought it to me whenever you started at Netherfield," she said. "Muriel would know that I'd get the answer right away."

"What *is* the answer then?" Neil asked, shivering in the cold.

"The answer is 'Black Bull'."

"A black bull?" Neil repeated, thinking the wind had blown her words away and he hadn't heard her properly.

"Yes," she nodded, pulling the paper from her pocket and showing him it. "Look!"

"I don't understand at all," his eyes mirrored his disbelief. "How do you get a black bull out of that?"

"Not *a* black bull, Neil. Just two words — Black Bull." She smiled at him. "You're obviously not a puzzle-solver. It's quite easy, really! Look, the first letter of each word reading downwards make up the words."

A gust of wind almost tore the paper from Mrs Weston's hands as she said this but she clung on to it and held it steady. The words positively jumped out at Neil as he read down the line. "Black Bull," he read. "How ... how didn't I see that before," he gasped, looking up at her in amazement. "I can't believe I missed it!"

"Have you been there yet?" she asked.

"Been where?" he queried.

"Why, to the Black Bull, of course," she answered with a smile, seeing his blank look.

"I've ... I've never even heard of it!"

She frowned and then her face cleared. "Of course," she said, "I'd quite forgotten that you haven't lived here for all that long. I ... well, I thought Muriel might have taken you there when you visited her. Your mum and dad will know it. They do an excellent lunch."

"So Mum and Dad will know where it is?"

"Bound to, I should think. It's a very old inn,"

she explained, "in a village called Etal — not all that
far away, as the crow flies, really, just a few miles."

"So ... so the Black Bull is actually a place ...?"
Neil's heart lifted. "For a few minutes I thought
I was going to have to go round the countryside
looking for black bulls!"

Mrs Weston shook her head. "Etal is well worth
a visit," she smiled. "It's very, very old, you know.
You'll like it. There's an ancient castle in the
middle of the village and the Black Bull's been
around for centuries! It has a thatched roof and,"
she paused, eyeing him with a smile and dropping
her voice to whisper softly in his ear, "there's an
old fireplace in the bar."

The Wind Witch who had been hovering round
them, frowned in annoyance. Try as she might,
she hadn't caught that last bit of the conversation
but maybe it wasn't so important. What she'd
already heard was enough to set her pulses racing.
Indeed, she was almost falling off her broomstick
in excitement at what she'd just heard. Just *wait*
until she told Wanda! Quivering with excitement,
she pulled up the handle of her broomstick and
soared towards the clouds.

It was as she had thought. At the mention of what
she'd discovered, she had her mistress's undivided
attention. Indeed, at first, Wanda, Queen of the
Wind Witches, could hardly believe her ears. A
human child holding the secret to the talisman! It
was unheard of! "Are you sure?" she said, sitting
up straight, her eyes sharp with interest.

The wind witch bowed low. This was her moment
of triumph! "The teacher mentioned Muriel,

Majesty," she said, "and I remembered that was Merial's name in the human world. I think the boy must be her nephew. I saw him in the garden at Craiglaw House when we were searching in the trees."

Wanda nodded impatiently. "And?"

"His name is Neil. That's what the teacher called him. Then she gave him the answer to a riddle."

"A riddle?" the queen repeated.

"That's what she called it. I tried to grab the paper out of her hand but I wasn't quick enough. She was holding on to it too tightly."

"But you read it?" the Queen asked anxiously.

"Of course, I read it, Majesty. I can't remember it word for word but it mentioned the talisman and the Lords of Morven."

"The Lords of Morven," Wanda sat back in the cushioned folds of her cloud-like throne and felt a stab of worry. One didn't meddle in the affairs of powerful magicians without good cause. But then, as far as she was concerned, the talisman was the best of causes. She brought her mind back swiftly to the present. "What was the answer to the riddle? Did you hear that?"

"I did, Majesty. The answer is Black Bull," the witch replied and, seeing her mistress's puzzled frown, added. "The boy didn't know what it meant either until she told him. It's the old inn at Etal. The Black Bull."

The queen rose gracefully from her throne, her grey silk robes falling in elegant folds round her feet. Her eyes shone with elation. "You have done very well, Janetta," she smiled, "very well, indeed. But you must tell no one about this." Her expression changed suddenly as she thought of what would happen should the Snow Witches get to hear of this boy; or the Earth Witches for that matter. "It must be our secret, do you understand?"

"I will tell no one, Majesty!" Janetta replied, reading the threat in the queen's glance.

"We will go to Etal tomorrow," the queen mused, already dreaming of the power the talisman would give her, "and you, Janetta, will be my second in command."

"Thank you, Majesty," Janetta curtseyed, her eyes shining with excitement.

The Queen smiled. "After all," she pointed out, "you are the only one who knows what this boy, Neil, looks like."

17. Halloween horror

"Better bring the umbrellas in as well while you're out there, Bert," Christine called out after him as a gust of wind swept in through the open door of the Black Bull, bringing with it a rustling scatter of dead leaves that lay in shades of brown, yellow and scarlet over the polished floorboards.

"Right," he said, closing the door behind him with an effort. The wind, however, was so strong that it jerked the handle from his hand and once more the door flew open letting in yet more streams of autumn leaves. With a gale like this blowing, he thought, finally managing to shut it, the trees would be stripped bare in no time and it was so cold that he doubted if anyone would be sitting outside to eat any time soon. Halloween or no Halloween, Christine was right. It was definitely time to put the outside furniture into store, umbrellas and all.

Inside the Black Bull, Christine listened to the howl of the wind and shivered suddenly. It was a dull, grey day and without the sun, the inside of the bar had become dark and strangely oppressive. She tried to shrug the feeling off but the underlying malevolence lingered in the air and frightened her considerably although she was loath to admit it.

There was also the uncanny feeling that she was being watched. She looked round nervously. Was there an intruder? She could see no one. Surely, she thought doubtfully, surely it wasn't her witches who were watching her ... for hanging here, there and everywhere, all over the bar and the dining area, was her collection of witches. They were her pride and joy. Some she'd bought herself but over the years, most of the others had been given to her as gifts. Indeed, it was amazing how the number had grown — for now at least thirty witches of all shapes and sizes decorated the bar.

Sitting astride a variety of broomsticks, they were beautifully dressed, their black cloaks stiffened with wire so that they flew out behind them. Some were young and reasonably pretty as witches go, with frothy petticoats and gaily striped stockings relieving the gloom of their outfits but most were repulsive old hags dressed in black with hooked plaster noses, pointed chins and droopy pointed hats.

Christine bit her lip for, witches apart, the place actually looked frighteningly ghoulish. She'd put a lot of work into the Halloween decorations and what with grinning pumpkins, green-eyed black cats and flapping, white ghosts, the room looked ... really creepy. Maybe, she thought, maybe they'd gone just a bit over the top with the decorations ...

"Christine!" She heard the chef's voice with an overwhelming sense of relief and turned thankfully to the warmth and brightness of the kitchen, anxious to leave her fears behind.

It was the mirror that hung at the side of the

kitchen door that gave them away and, for an instant, her heart stopped beating — for the minute she turned her back on them, they started moving. Her witches! They were real and alive, their cloaks swirling, their eyes gleaming nastily and their frowning, painted faces, masks of evil.

She swung round and they immediately froze. Her eyes strayed to the front door. It was closed. Bert had shut it and there was no draught. Being a down-to-earth, sensible woman, however, she clung obstinately to reason. It was ridiculous, she told herself frantically, how could the witches move?

She looked at her favourite witch, a really wicked-looking old hag with gorgeously made clothes that hung at the end of the bar and its eyes met hers with an evil malevolence that sent her stepping backwards with a cry of fear.

"You all right, Christine?" queried the chef, grabbing her arm. "You nearly tripped on the step, there."

"It's the witches," she whispered, her face as white as a sheet. "I thought ... I thought for a moment that they were ... alive."

Chef gave her a funny look. If he hadn't known that Christine didn't drink, he'd have sworn she'd been at the brandy. "Don't be daft," he said, sounding irritated. He'd just found out that they needed green coriander for the curry, which meant a trip into Berwick and he wasn't, therefore, in the best of tempers. "Now," he said, propelling her briskly back into the bar, "what's the problem?"

She couldn't believe it. The bar was totally normal, the awful atmosphere had gone and her witches hung innocently on their invisible strings; just as they'd always done. Relief swept through her. "Thanks," she sniffed, reaching for a tissue and blowing her nose loudly, "I can't think *what* got into me!"

"You don't fancy a trip into Berwick, do you?" he asked hopefully. "We've run out of green coriander and there are a few other things I could stock up on ..."

"No problem," Christine seized on the chance to get out of the bar and, remembering a sweater she'd seen in a shop in Marygate the previous week, decided that a bit of retail therapy was decidedly in order. "Make me a list and I'll get my bag," she said, feeling a million times more cheerful.

Chef stood in the bar as she went to get her coat and handbag. He didn't share his employer's passion for plaster witches any more than her husband did. "Bleedin' witches!" he said aloud as he turned back to the kitchen.

Then he stopped dead and very slowly turned to look again at the witch that hung near the till; a rather dashing young witch that sported a frothy white petticoat under her striped dress. The witch looked blandly back at him with just a touch of amusement in her black eyes. He swallowed. Just another plaster witch or ... was it? Now *he* was at it, he thought wildly, returning to the kitchen ... imagining things ...

Nevertheless, as he picked up a meat cleaver and proceeded to attack an inoffensive joint with unaccustomed vigour, he was pretty sure that he hadn't been mistaken — for as he'd turned, he could have sworn that the witch had winked at him.

18. All Hallow's Eve

The MacLeans arrived in Etal at around six o'clock in the evening. It was Halloween, the night was as black as pitch and the Black Bull, when they reached it, was already quite busy. The parking space at the front was full, with lots more cars parked down the side of the road.

"They must be having a Halloween party for the children," Mrs MacLean remarked, for the outside of the Black Bull was strung with white cardboard ghosts and huge pumpkin lanterns glowed from its windows. As his father drove past the line of cars, looking for an empty space, Neil peered out of the window on the other side and found himself looking at the massive ruins of an old castle.

"Look over there, Clara! That must be the ruin Mrs Weston told me about."

"We'll have to visit it one day," Mrs MacLean said, craning her neck to peer at it as they drove past.

The car was now driving slowly down a steep hill and the headlights, on full beam, picked up the glint of water.

"There's a river down there, by the looks of things," Clara said. "Can you park, Dad, so we can have a look?"

There was a turning place by the river, lit by a lonely lamp. Despite the cold, they got out of the car and stood beside the swiftly flowing water that rushed, tumbled and frothed over boulders and drifts of pebbles.

"It's a ford, isn't it," Clara said. "The water looks quite shallow."

"Yeah, I bet you could walk over, no problem," Neil said confidently, measuring up the distance to the bank on the other side of the river. "It's not that far, really."

His father looked at him sideways. "Rubbish, Neil," he said briskly. "Use your eyes. Can't you see the current? It would sweep you off your feet before you'd taken a few steps."

"I suppose," Neil muttered.

"Listen to me, Neil!" his father grasped him by the shoulders and turned him round to face him. "Rivers aren't swimming pools! They can be deceptive and dangerous; especially rivers that are deep and slow moving. They're the worst, because you can't see the currents below the surface of the water. You don't *ever* swim in them, do you understand? I'm serious, Neil," he added. "Don't *ever* forget what I've just told you!"

"Okay, Dad." Neil didn't argue. He knew by the sound of his father's voice that it was advice to take to heart.

They stood for a while longer, watching the water tumbling past until Janet shivered and hugged her coat round her. "Can we go up to the Black Bull now?" she pleaded. "It's more than a bit chilly down here."

"Pile in, then," her husband grinned. "I'll try and find a parking place further up the road. Now, does everyone know what to do?"

"Clara and I become invisible and try to find the talisman by the fireplace while you order dinner," Neil said. "Then Clara and I go out, switch our rings and come back in, whether we've found the talisman or not. Perfectly simple!"

"Actually, I didn't expect the Black Bull to be so full," his father said, changing gear. "I totally forgot about Halloween and if there's a party on ... well, it might be better if you came in with us, Neil, and let Clara look for the talisman on her own. If I remember rightly, the fireplace isn't that big and there are tables quite close to it."

"That's true," Janet MacLean nodded as the car pulled into an empty space. "There's more chance of somebody bumping into you if there are two of you. You don't mind, do you, Neil?"

"No," Neil said at once, "I suppose it'll be safer if she's on her own."

"Ready to switch rings, Clara?" her dad said. "Better do it now. No one's around to see you."

The Black Bull was warm, comfortable and noisy for there was, indeed, a party going on and the place was full of children in Halloween costumes. Fortunately, an elderly couple got up to leave as they entered and John MacLean moved quickly towards the empty table. Pity it wasn't nearer the fireplace, he thought, for, although invisible, he wanted to keep as much of an eye as he could, on Clara.

Looking round casually, he saw the horde of plaster witches that decorated the room. Some of them were beautifully made and certainly collectors' items. Handy decorations to have, he thought idly, when Halloween came round.

"This is nice," Janet MacLean said, settling herself into a chair and handing round the menus. "Now, let's see what they have to offer. What do you fancy, Neil?"

"Your mother's talking to you, Neil," his father said, looking up from his menu. Then he saw Neil's face, white and staring. "What is it?" he asked. "What's the matter?"

"Can't you feel them?" Neil whispered harshly.

"Feel what?" John MacLean asked.

"Witches," Neil said abruptly. "The place is full of them!"

"Yes, they're lovely aren't they," his mother agreed, smiling. "They belong to the owner's wife. She must have added quite a few to her collection since we were last here, don't you think, John? There are a lot more than I remember."

Neil looked at his parents in complete disbelief as realization dawned. "You're not wearing your firestones, are you?" he said furiously.

"Well, no," his mother admitted, glancing at her husband. "We didn't think we'd need them."

"I *don't* believe it!" Neil said, sitting back in his seat, totally appalled. "How on *earth* could you think you wouldn't need them? Listen," he whispered, leaning forward across the narrow little table, "this room is full of witches! Real witches! I can sense them. They're hiding in the plaster models. Don't look, for goodness sake!" he said as his mother's eyes strayed to a nearby witch.

"Calm down, Neil. They won't be able to see Clara," his father said, looking casually towards the fireplace at the end of the room. All the tables there were occupied but a waitress was moving backwards and forwards with plates of food and one of the couples had children. The little girl had a cat-suit on but the boy was older and, making the most of a white ghost costume, was prancing round the place making *whoooeeee* noises.

"That boy could trip over Clara any minute," his mother said worriedly, watching his antics.

Neil pushed his chair back. "There are loads of old pictures on the wall beside the fireplace," he whispered. "I'll pretend to be looking at them and try and keep that awful kid clear of Clara."

A ripple of excitement swept the witches as Neil got to his feet. Janetta had been quick to pass the word round. This was the boy they were looking for. He'd come to find the talisman! The witches' eyes followed him as he made his way towards the end of the room where the fire burned brightly. Clara saw him coming and as he stopped to look at an old picture of the inn taken at least a hundred years ago, she whispered in his ear. "This place is full of witches!"

"I know," he said, his voice drowned by the din of the party, "and would you believe it, Mum and Dad aren't wearing their firestones!"

"Seriously? What were they thinking?"

"Goodness knows. Have you found anything?"

"Well, there's a loose brick down there on the right. I think that might be it but it's a bit too stiff for me to move," Clara breathed softly. "It'll take time but don't worry, I'll get it eventually."

It was then that Neil remembered Miss Markham's words as she'd left the library. "It'll come to me eventually," she'd said. Maybe that was it, thought Neil. Maybe she'd been using the spell to hex the talisman to her — maybe that was why the brick was loose ...

"Move over a bit," he hissed, "I'll have a go ..."

"But what about the witches?" breathed Clara. "They must know it's hidden in here somewhere!"

"Yeah, but they don't know who we are and they certainly don't know that *you're* here," Neil pointed out. "Look, if I find it, I'll give it to you right away, okay?"

"Okay," Clara agreed.

Neil bent down over the fireplace and jiggled the brick while Clara stood guard beside him. Nobody was really interested in what he was doing, she thought, looking round. Most people would think he was just warming his hands by the fire and a couple sitting nearby had given him no more than a casual glance before returning to their conversation.

The brick came free with a sudden jerk and Neil tumbled backwards as a small, square black box fell out of the hole; a small, square box with a strange silver design on its lid. The talisman! It must be!

The witches exploded from their hiding places in the plaster witches with a force that shattered them into fragments. The noise was deafening and the green miasma of smoke that hung in the air smelled vaguely of rotten eggs. This, coupled with the witches' sudden appearance, terrified everyone in the room. Evil radiated from them and children ran screaming to their mothers who clutched at them protectively.

Christine looked blankly at the real witches. Clad as they were in dingy, grey silk with evil faces, black cloaks and black droopy hats they were nothing like the beautiful models that she'd collected so lovingly over the years. All that was left of them were tangled bundles of torn material for not one of her treasures remained intact. As she gazed at their shattered remains, fury rose inside her and such was her anger that the witches, who were truly terrifying, had no power to frighten her. Simmering with rage, she backed slowly into the kitchen to organize Bert and the chef. She'd show them!

Most people had, for the first few seconds at least, taken the appearance of the witches as a stunt dreamt up by Christine and Bert and one or two couples even started to clap. The clapping, however, swiftly petered out as the witches took over. Confusion reigned as some old hags, their faces masks of evil, leapt nimbly upwards to crouch threateningly on high shelving and protruding beams. No one dared move with the witches' eyes constantly watching them and the MacLeans were given special treatment. They were, after all, the parents of the boy, Neil. Even as John MacLean, looking anxiously at his wife, put his napkin on the table and made to get to his feet, a couple of witches slid into the seats beside them. Janet froze but one look at the witches' faces told them that they could do nothing to help Neil. They eyed one another worriedly. At least Clara was invisible ...

Wanda, Queen of the Wind Witches, seeing that she had everything under control, raised her arms. Silence fell as she stepped forward in a rustle of grey silk to confront Neil who had scrambled to his feet.

The witch held out her hand, imperiously. "Give me the talisman!" she demanded.

Neil put his hands behind his back instinctively. He'd seen the box disappear as Clara had grabbed it so it didn't really matter what happened now. The talisman was safe.

"Give it to me, Neil!" the queen repeated impatiently. The boy had to have it, she thought. There was nobody near him and she'd seen the box fall into the hearth with her own eyes.

"Why should I give it to you?" he asked, wondering how on earth she knew his name. And then he remembered the wind that had been blowing over the playing field when Mrs Weston had shown him the answer to the riddle. He hadn't been wearing his firestone because he'd had his sports kit on but the witches must have been there, flying around unseen. And they were Wind Witches, he knew. Wasn't it Jaikie who had said they always wore grey?

"Give it to me — now, at once!" Wanda demanded.

"I don't have it," he parried.

"I saw it!" Wanda snapped. "Now, hand it over!"

Neil shook his head.

"Perhaps," she said viciously, "you would like me to hex you?"

Neil paled but he knew he had to give Clara time to get away. The trouble was that with the arrival of the witches, the room was full to overflowing. It would take Clara ages to sneak her way through the crowd to get anywhere near the door.

Neil drew his hands as slowly as he could from behind his back and then turned up his palms so that she could see that he held nothing.

The witches hissed in fury. Wanda raised her arm and a deathly silence fell. Neil knew she was going to hex him and taking a deep breath, met her eyes defiantly, hoping fervently that the MacArthur's spell would protect him.

"Give – me – the – talisman!" she grated. "Now!"

"I ... I dropped it in the fire," Neil said quickly. He hadn't, of course, and she knew he hadn't.

It was just as she opened her mouth to hex him that Christine, Bert and the chef went into action. Barging in through side doors with full soda siphons in each hand, they pressed the levers and sent powerful jets of fizzy water straight into the witches' faces. It didn't do them any harm but in seconds they reduced the room to a scene of total confusion as, gasping and spluttering, the witches were knocked sideways.

"Through here! Quick!" Christine yelled, holding the door open and, as Neil shot through, she locked it smartly behind him.

Clara almost made it to the door ... but not quite. It was Bert's fault although he didn't mean it. On a complete high, Bert was having the time of his life, aiming the jets of water at all the witches he could see when Clara got in the way. As the jet of water hit her, she remembered Lady Ellan's words. "You'll be fine," she'd said, "as long as you don't go walking under any waterfalls. The magic shield goes to pieces in anything heavier than rain." Clara looked round in horror as the magic shield that encircled her, shimmered and faded.

The witches spotted her immediately. One of them screamed and as they all turned to stare in the direction of her pointing finger, Clara's heart sank like a stone. She'd been seen! Throwing caution to the winds, she pushed her way through the last of the crowd, made it to the door and darted swiftly through.

"Get her!" Wanda screeched.

The witches let out a hungry, howling cry that froze the blood and made a concerted rush for the door. It was to prove their undoing for in their anxiety to catch Clara they all landed in the doorway at more or less the same time and quite successfully jammed the opening. Precious seconds were lost in the violent struggle that ensued and by the time they finally managed to get clear, Clara had a flying start.

Fear lent her wings as, clutching the box tightly, she raced down the steep hill towards the river with a screaming horde of witches streaming after her.

19. Race for the river

As Clara flew down the steep hill towards the river, Auntie Murial's words echoed through her mind. "Witches can't cross running water, Clara." And then there were her father's words, spoken just a short time ago. "Can't you see the current, Neil ... it would sweep you off your feet before you took a few steps."

Panting for breath, she stopped by the water's edge and knew that if she were going to escape, she had to cross it. Stuffing the talisman securely down the front of her jacket, she zipped it up firmly and, casting a frantic look over her shoulder, saw that the witches were closing in fast.

Turning again to the swiftly flowing river, she stiffened in fright as an old man appeared suddenly from the shadows. "Don't be afraid, Clara," he said, with half an eye on the approaching witches. "Give me the talisman and I'll take you across the river."

His voice sounded vaguely familiar but Clara had no time to think. "Who are you?" she asked.

"Give me the talisman," he demanded urgently. "I need it! Please! Give it to me! Quickly, or the witches will catch you!"

Clara swung round and sure enough, the witches were already more than halfway down the brae.

The sight of them was enough! Totally petrified, she ignored the pleas of the old man and heedless of danger, left him standing. Splashing into the sweeping current, she fixed her eyes on the far bank and didn't see him draw back into the shadows as the witches approached, nor see the despair that lined his face. His powers were fading, there were too many of them to hex — but if Clara didn't make it across the river then he still had a chance to get the talisman ... there *had* to be a chance, he thought desperately, or his life would soon be over ...

Clara felt the pull of the current the minute she hit the water. It was much stronger than she'd thought and the river wasn't nearly as shallow as she'd expected, either. Desperately, she half-waded and half-floundered towards the opposite bank until one of her trainers wedged between a couple of slimy boulders and gave her some welcome, if painful, support. She paused, panting, in what proved to be a small oasis of stillness amid the driving currents. The stones weren't all that big but, jutting just above the water, were large enough to part the sweeping, cascading flow of the river.

She reckoned she'd made it about a third of the way across and breathed a sigh of relief. At least the witches couldn't harm her now. They'd reached the water's edge and were crowding the river bank, totally frustrated and furious at her escape.

Again, she looked ahead to the opposite bank. As Neil had said, it wasn't that far but she knew from the force of the river that she'd never make it. If she tried, she'd be carried away downstream and although she'd stuffed the box with the talisman in it, down the front of her jacket, she knew she might lose it in the river if she were to fall in.

Desperately, she glanced behind her again, hoping that the witches might have given up on her. No such luck, she thought, they were still there. So, too, she noticed, were the people from the Black Bull, a motley crew in their Halloween outfits for, after the witches' hurried exit, the MacLeans had not only shot out after them but the whole of the pub had followed suit, anxious not to miss out on the most exciting event that had happened in the village in years.

Even as she watched, her father appeared among the witches, shoving them aside as he pushed his way to the front of the crowd and, with the water lapping at his feet, cupped his hands to his mouth and yelled across the river. "Put the talisman on, Clara!" he shouted. *"Put it on!"*

"How could I have been so *stupid*?" Clara thought as she waved to show that she'd understood. Quickly, she pulled down the zipper of her jacket and muttered as it stuck halfway down. "Come on, open," she muttered, furiously. As it refused to budge, she gave up the struggle and stuck her hand inside. Even as she touched the box, the lid opened and she felt the cold metal of a broad bangle. Although she had meant to lift it out of its box, the talisman itself seemed to have other ideas — for the minute her hand touched it, it slipped swiftly over her wrist.

There was a horrified scream of despair from the witches as, pulling back the sleeve of her jacket, Clara held her arm high above her head so that everyone could see the shining band of silver round her arm.

Ignoring the witches, the old man stepped forward from the shadow of the trees and, arm outstretched, sent the hex flying across the river in a desperate attempt to take the talisman for himself. Indeed, had Clara been holding it in her hand, he might well have succeeded but as it was, the hex struck her arm with vicious force, sparked off the talisman in a blaze of light and knocked her into the river.

Neil swung round just in time to see a decrepit-looking old man standing by the water's edge, before he vanished from sight. A magician! But who could it possibly be? The witches, too, had seen him and, drawing back warily, eyed their queen. Wanda was grinding her teeth in rage as she saw her plan to take the talisman fall apart but nevertheless knew better than to interfere in the affairs of magicians. Her face was a mask of fury as, lifting her arm, she gave the signal to withdraw and Neil watched in amazement as the grey-clad witches shivered, dimmed and faded away.

"The witches have gone, Dad," he said excitedly, pulling at his arm, and then fell silent as he followed his father's gaze. A gasp of amazement had risen from the crowd. It was unbelievable. The river had stopped running.

Clara, herself, couldn't understand what had happened. Why wasn't she in the river? She half-scrambled to her feet and looked around. All of a sudden, there was no water. Admittedly, the ground around her was stony and wet. Boulders and a myriad of rounded pebbles gleamed in the dim light of the solitary lamp post on the bank but the river had gone. It was only when she turned that she realized what had happened. The river had stopped flowing and she was facing a huge wave of water that loomed over her, growing higher with every second that passed.

"Clara!" Her father scrunched across the boulder-strewn bed of the river towards her and grabbed her by the arm. "Come on," he said urgently, shaking her out of her daze. "It must be the talisman that's holding the water back! Come on, run for it!" And together they ran back to the safety of the bank.

It wasn't far and everyone cheered. It was a cheer that tailed off and petered out, however, as all eyes then turned back to the enormous wave that had built up. It was an amazing sight and several seconds were to pass before it finally reared high in the air and then crashed down with a violence that sent a huge surge of brown water tumbling crazily down the river.

"The witches have gone, Bert," Christine said, looking round in relief, half-wondering if she'd imagined them.

"Good riddance," her husband muttered as, like everyone else, they turned to walk with the MacLeans, back up the slope towards the Black Bull. "I'm sorry about your witches, though, love," he added quietly, remembering the look of devastation on his wife's face when she'd seen the ragged remains of her collection. "You'll just have to start all over again and build up another lot, eh!"

Christine looked at him fondly. She knew he'd never liked her witches but, give him his due, he'd never said a word against them. "You're a good man, Bert," she said, with a grin, "but, you know, I seem to have gone off witches completely! In fact, it wouldn't worry me if I were never to see another witch again in my whole life."

20. Cross words

Neil and Clara cringed at the tone of his voice and even their parents looked uncomfortable. There was no doubt about it: the MacArthur was furious with them. His face was grim and his voice was icy. "Kitor and Cassia," he nodded towards the two crows who perched on the arm of Hamish's chair, "told me how you went on your own inside the witches' castle and stole *The Book of Spells.*" He took a deep breath. "Quite frankly, I almost had heart failure at the very thought."

Hamish and Jaikie nodded in agreement. They'd been fairly gobsmacked themselves when Kitor had told them what Neil and Clara had been up to. Thank goodness they'd come out of it in one piece! Even Arthur breathed a disapproving cloud of smoke down his long nose.

"*Why* did you do it, Neil?" The MacArthur threw a worried glance at their parents who were sitting to the right of his chair. "What on earth got into you to undertake such a dangerous task on your own? Your father tells me that you didn't even tell *him* what you were going to do." He threw up his hands disbelievingly. "Didn't you realize the danger you were in? Maritza, the Queen of the Earth Witches, is a nasty bit of work! How many

times do I have to tell you! The witches are evil!
We warned you, didn't we?"

Maritza! Clara gulped and looked apprehensively
at Neil. It had been bad enough finding out that
their drama teacher was a witch but to learn
that she was actually Queen of the Earth Witches
was totally mind-boggling! A warning glance and
a slight shake of the head from Neil, however,
kept her quiet. What their parents didn't know
wouldn't hurt them.

"Well, yes," Neil admitted, "I know. You did tell
us that they were evil but, you see, you'd put a
spell on our firestones and we had our magic rings
on so we thought we'd be ... all right." He tailed
off at the frowning look of despair the MacArthur
gave him.

"All right!" the MacArthur repeated, looking
round the assembled gathering. "You thought
you'd be all right, did you?" he continued, holding
up the black leather book with its design of
mystical symbols on the cover. He laid it once more
on his lap and shook his head in despair. "Don't
you realize what you've done?"

Neil looked sideways at Clara and shook his head.

"You," the MacArthur snapped, glaring at them,
"out of total, complete, utterly abyssmal ignorance,
have just pulled off the biggest robbery there will
ever be in the world of magic! Absolutely the
biggest!" he said, breathing deeply. He shook his
head. "How the witches came to have it in their
library, I'll never know," he continued, "for it's
been lost for centuries and the spells it contains
are ancient. My theory is that someone, in ages

past, deliberately hid it very well. And rightly so, for as well as being the oldest book in the world, it's also the most dangerous." He gazed down at it and as his finger traced the pentagram that decorated the cover, he looked up and added in a more reasonable tone. "The only good thing to come out of all this is that at least you had the sense to bring it here." He handed the heavy volume to Jaikie who laid it reverently on a side table. "To bring it here *eventually*, I should say," he glowered, for the thought of *The Book of Spells* lying unprotected on the top of Clara's wardrobe at school was enough to give anyone nightmares! "And as if *that* weren't enough," he continued, his voice rising, "what does Clara do but waltz in here on her magic carpet, pull up her sleeve and show us Lady Merial's talisman!! Now *do* tell me!" he demanded, "when on earth did *this* happen? *How* did you manage to find the talisman?" A sudden thought struck him and he turned his head to stare suspiciously at Kitor and Cassia.

The two crows, totally stunned at the MacArthur's irate tirade, shook their heads.

"Kitor and Cassia knew nothing about it," Clara assured him, following his glance. "You see, one of Neil's teachers solved the riddle and we thought ..."

"You didn't think!" the MacArthur interrupted crossly, "you haven't thought at all throughout this whole affair! That's the trouble!"

Hamish, Jaikie and Archie looked at one another sideways and decided to keep their heads down and their mouths shut. Even Arthur rolled his wonderful eyes and made do with a painfully discreet cloud of smoke.

John MacLean took a deep breath and told the MacArthur the whole story of their trip to the Black Bull. "I'm really sorry," he apologised. "I should have told you the minute Neil found the answer to the riddle. After what happened, we all realize that we should have asked your advice."

"We thought it'd be easy, you see," Neil chipped in. "I'd no idea that the Wind Witches were listening to what Mrs Weston was saying."

Clara nodded agreement. "Don't be so cross with us, MacArthur," she pleaded. "We thought ..." her voice quavered for a second, "we thought it'd be a piece of cake. We'd use our rings, become invisible, find the talisman and nobody in the Black Bull would be any the wiser ..."

"Instead of which," another voice interrupted, sounding distinctly amused, "you seem to have set the world of magic in a spin! What *have* the pair of you been up to? Father sounded *most* mysterious!"

"Lady Ellan," Clara shrieked, running towards the pretty fair-haired young woman who had just stepped from the huge magic mirror that stood to the left of her father's great chair.

"Lord Rothlan!" John MacLean breathed a sigh of relief as a slim, kilted figure clutching a long, fur-lined robe round him, also emerged from the mirror. The huge eagle, perched on his shoulders, spread his wings as they entered the cavern and swooped to land beside Clara.

"Amgarad!" she said happily. "Oh, Amgarad, it's great to see you again."

Hamish, Jaikie and Archie rose to their feet and

a delighted Arthur, blowing streams of fire into the air, managed to contain himself long enough to bow to Lady Ellan and her husband. As far as he was concerned, there couldn't have been more welcome visitors and he wasn't alone in hoping that the sight of his daughter and son-in-law might put the MacArthur in a better temper.

By the time greetings were exchanged, the MacArthur had thawed noticeably but his manner was still cool and, despite Lady Ellan's teasing, he refused to let the matter of the witches, rest.

"You must always," he said brusquely to Neil and Clara, "let me know when you plan anything dangerous so that I can take steps to protect you. The witches are ... are ..." he threw his hands out, lost for words.

"They're a nasty lot," Jaikie said, risking a comment. "If they'd hexed you ..."

"They did hex me," Clara admitted, "but I was wearing the talisman by then and it saved me."

Neil looked at his sister in surprise. "No, they didn't," he corrected her.

"Come off it, Neil," she looked at him questioningly, "you were *there*! You *know* they did!" She turned to her father. *"Didn't* they, Dad?"

"But you're wrong, Clara," Neil insisted. "It wasn't the witches that hexed you. Honestly!"

Everyone, including his father and mother, looked at him in surprise. "Not the witches?" Clara echoed, looking slightly stunned. "Then who was it?"

"Yes, who?" his father asked, puzzled. "There was no one else there to hex her."

"Yes, there was," Neil declared. "I only caught

a glimpse of him," he admitted, looking round the little group, "but I saw him quite clearly. It was an old man with straggly, grey hair."

So puzzled were they at Neil's words that the MacLeans didn't notice the look of surprised understanding that flashed between Lord Rothlan and the MacArthur, but Jaikie picked up on it and looked thoughtful.

"Oh, him!" Clara said, oblivious to the sensation she was causing. "He was standing beside the river when I ran down the slope. "He ..." she paused and looked thoughtful. "Right enough," she said slowly, "he knew who I was." She looked at the MacArthur. "He called me Clara and he knew I had the talisman. He ... he asked me for it."

"*Asked* you for it!" Neil expostulated. "That was a bit of a cheek, wasn't it?"

Clara frowned. "He said he needed it ..."

"Well, *he* was the one who hexed you," Neil rejoined, "and, d'you know, I can't help thinking that I've seen him somewhere before ... but I can't remember where."

The MacArthur, watching his face crease in puzzlement, made no comment and quickly decided that this was an excellent time to reveal *The Book of Spells*. Knowing just how much of a sensation it was going to cause, it would not only serve to divert attention from the identity of the old man but would also give Lord Rothlan the surprise of his life. He smiled slightly and, hiding his excitement, whispered to Jaikie.

Lord Rothlan stiffened slightly at the sight of the book in Jaikie's arms but it was only when he put it down carefully in front of him that he realized what he was looking at.

The MacArthur beamed. The result was everything that he'd hoped for. Lord Rothlan looked dumbfounded and Lady Ellan stared in complete astonishment. They both knew immediately what it was, for the book was a thing of legend and famous throughout the world of magic.

"The Book of Spells!" Lord Rothlan breathed in amazement, his fingers tracing the gold pentagram that decorated the black leather cover. "Where on earth did you get this?" he demanded, his eyes bright with excitement as he opened the book carefully and, turning over some of the pages, looked in awe at the pictures of trolls, daemons and other magical creatures that covered them. "Yes," he said in a voice tinged with wonder, "this is definitely it! *The Book of Spells!*"

"Who wrote it?" Clara whispered.

"A wizard wrote it" he breathed, "a *great* wizard wrote it!" He glanced quickly at the MacArthur as he turned back to the first page. The parchment, yellow with age, was adorned with twining leaves in shades of green and gold but the inscription in the middle, shone clearly in a flowing red script: *Written by Astar Imeral.* "Legend always had it that the book was written by an ancient wizard called Imeral," Rothlan said, "and now we know that the legend was correct."

"Imeral," Lady Ellan explained, "lived somewhere in the middle of Europe. Over the years, he recorded all the spells he had learned in his lifetime so that they'd never be forgotten. He was always afraid, though, that the book might be stolen by other magicians so he kept it in the topmost tower of his castle. Powerful spells guarded the stairway and for many years he managed to keep it safe. But word got around and ..."

"... it was stolen by a huge bird," the MacArthur finished matter-of-factly. "It flew in through the window of the tower and carried it away in its claws. And from then on," he added, "it disappeared and hasn't been seen since ... until now, that is."

"Over the years, some of the spells filtered out, mind you," Rothlan pointed out. "Everyone knew where they came from because of the language they were written in — but no one ever admitted to stealing the book!"

Lady Ellan turned and looked at her father. "Well," she said expectantly, "aren't you going to tell us where you found it?"

The MacArthur nodded towards Neil and Clara. "Ask the pair of them," he advised, and he smiled wryly as he said it.

There was a sudden silence as Lord Rothlan and Lady Ellan looked at them in amazement. *"You!"* Lord Rothlan said, looking at them blankly. *"You* found the book?"

"They didn't find it," the MacArthur snapped. "They *stole* it from the Earth Witches' castle!"

"Stole it!" Lady Ellan's eyes widened in disbelief and her voice rose by a couple of octaves. *"From the witches*! You ... you *didn't!"* Her eyes flew from Neil to Clara and back again.

It was then that Neil realized the enormity of what they'd done and the terrible risks they'd taken to get hold of the book. He looked at Clara, suddenly frightened. Had the witches caught them, he thought, they'd probably have hexed them to bits!

"Why even I, with all my magic ..." Lady Ellan's voice petered out as her husband nudged her gently.

"Why don't we all sit down and you can tell us exactly what happened," Lord Rothlan said calmly. And it was only once they were comfortably settled that Neil then told the story of their escapade inside the witches' castle and while everyone listened, fascinated, Clara looked down at *The Book of Spells*. Lord Rothlan had opened it to reveal a page covered in ornate red script that glowed like fresh blood on the yellowish parchment. No one noticed her face change; they were all too busy listening to Neil. Before, when she'd read the book in her room at school, she hadn't understood the strange language but now, with the talisman on her arm, she realized that she understood every word. The knowedge that she now had the power to call up daemons, spectres, efrites and a host of other strange creatures whose names she had never heard of before, made her shiver. She had seen their pictures in the book and knew what they looked like and where they lurked. Some of them were the stuff of nightmares.

She looked up and met Arthur's wonderful eyes. A look of understanding passed between them and she suddenly realized that things had changed. She was no longer on the fringe of the world of magic like Neil and her parents.

She was now part of it.

21. Pumpkin Pie

Neil looked appreciatively round the auditorium of the school's little theatre. It was buzzing with excited chatter as by this time most of the classes had filed in and everyone was more or less seated. Mrs Weston slipped into her seat at the end of the row and the other teachers, too, he noticed, had started to take their places, a sure sign that the play was due to start soon. His eyes sharpened as he noticed that Herr von Grozny, sitting with his form class, was in the row in front of him. A sudden flutter of worry made Neil frown. Nothing, surely, could go wrong with *Pumpkin Pie?*

If the truth be told, he'd felt uneasy ever since they'd got back from Edinburgh. Odd things bothered him. Clara, for a start; for despite the MacArthur's assurances that the protective hex he'd put round the talisman would mean that no one would sense its magic, she'd been worried at wearing it in school, pushing the clasp halfway up her arm so that her sweater would hide it. Neil sighed, knowing that the last couple of rehearsals had been a bit nerve-racking for her. However, Miss Markham didn't seem to have noticed anything and she wouldn't see von Grozny any time soon as her next German lesson wasn't until the following week.

She'll be fine, he told himself. After all, the witches would hardly try anything on during the play. Not, he reckoned, with the formidable Queen of the Earth Witches in the wings. No, he was letting his imagination run away with him. Anyway, what could possibly happen during a school play with the theatre full of teachers?

Then he remembered a few of his friends giggling with some of the third year boys. Something *was* going to happen, he thought suddenly. After putting half of them in detention at the start of the term, Miss Markham wasn't at all popular with the third year and he'd vaguely gathered that they were up to some sort of mischief. But was it connected with the play? Some of them had sisters in Clara's year — surely they wouldn't do anything to sabotage the performance? Looking behind him, however, he immediately had his suspicions confirmed. The third years were sitting quietly enough but there was an air of suppressed excitement about them that told him all he wanted to know ... and his heart sank ...

Just then, the lights dimmed and a spotlight blazed, illuminating the sinister, threatening figure of Miss Markham who slid evilly from behind the gold-tasselled, red velvet curtains. She had dressed for the occasion in witch's clothes and although she'd added a pair of rather daring, red and white striped stockings to her ensemble, her presence sent a frisson of unease round the audience. There was an immediate outbreak of hissing, which was quickly quelled by the staff and by Miss Markham herself as, with a furious glare round the hall, she welcomed them to the dress rehearsal of *Pumpkin Pie*.

Neil glanced quickly at the teachers that were within his range of vision and caught them exchanging rather startled glances. He felt sure that none of them had realized just how much the upper school disliked Miss Markham.

It was then that Neil caught sight of him, standing at the side of the auditorium, quite near Herr von Grozny; a small, elderly man with grey, straggly hair. The janitor, thought Neil, who had saved their skins when von Grozny had nearly caught them in the library. Funny, he hadn't seen him around since then. He looked at him again and almost choked as realization dawned. He *had* seen him again — at the river when he'd tried to hex Clara! The same old man! He *must* be a magician of some sort! But *who* was he?

Neil slumped back in his seat, quite oblivious to the gasps of wonder that ran round the auditorium as the curtains parted to reveal the witches' fantastic castle. It was huge and looked frighteningly creepy. Black paper bats flapped spookily round its grim battlements and an owl hooted eerily. The seniors sat up expectantly and even the teachers looked interested. Maybe the play was going to be worth watching after all.

Neil's mind, meanwhile, was racing frantically. Who on earth, he wondered worriedly, was the old man? He groaned. There was just *so* much he didn't *know*! As it happened, the old man was to prove the least of his problems. Although Miss Markham had no reason to suspect Clara, the Wind Witches knew what she looked like and putting two and two together, had gathered that the children to Netherfield, Lady Merial's old school. So, even as Neil sat in the audience, worrying his socks off, they were there already, perched high above the stage in the flies, waiting for a chance to grab the talisman.

The fly floor, in any theatre, soars at least thirty feet above the heads of the actors and is little more than a ten-foot platform jutting out round three sides of the stage. The Wind Witches, therefore, got the shock of their lives when the Snow Witches materialized on the opposite platform. Wanda looked distraught. How on earth did Samantha know about the children? She'd have sworn that no Snow Witches had been within spitting distance of Etal that night. Who had let the cat out of the bag? She glared round furiously but as every witch in her coven looked just as appalled as she did, she remained none the wiser.

What she couldn't know was that some of the Snow Witches *had* actually witnessed the incident at the ford and had not only seen Clara but had also passed the news of the event on to their mistress. Samantha had listened carefully and her instructions had been brief, clear and to the point. Since then, she and her coven had secretly followed the Wind Witches wherever they went and, although time-consuming, her tactics had paid off. Indeed, the look of stunned astonishment on Wanda's face when they'd turned up had been ample reward for their efforts!

Samantha, looking supremely confident in her shredded, silver gown, smiled sweetly and rejoiced inwardly at Wanda's hidden fury. Bowing mockingly from her perch on the platform opposite, she knew perfectly well that there wasn't a lot Wanda could do without revealing their presence to Maritza. Wanda inclined her head graciously in response and, holding her tongue and her temper, crouched in the heights above the stage, waiting for an opportunity — any opportunity — to grab the talisman before Samantha, or any of the other witches, had the chance to get their hands on it!

The play progressed amid bursts of laughter, gasps of horror and loud cheers from the audience for, as Clara had said, it was a good play. It wasn't until the second act, however, that Miss Markham unwittingly set the ball rolling.

The sleeves of Clara's witch outfit weren't, unfortunately, all that long and although she'd done her best to push the talisman up her arm, her sleeve fell back accidentally as she dipped a long-handled ladle in the cauldron and lifted out a huge black spider. As the audience went "Aaaarghhh", the talisman was revealed for all to see the shining clasp of silver round her arm blazing in the glare of the spotlights. Neil closed his eyes. Now she'd done it!

Standing in the prompt corner, still totally unaware of the witches crowding the flies above her head, the inevitable happened. Miss Markham spotted the talisman. Her mouth fell open and excitement gripped her like a vice. How or where this child had found the talisman, she didn't know, but within a very short time — like right now — it was going to be hers!

Several things then happened in quick succession. She strode onto the stage, pushing the girls roughly to one side in her anxiety to get to Clara. This, of course, wasn't in the original script but no one thought of protesting. Even the teachers in the audience were frozen to their seats. One look at her face was enough! Surely, this was a real witch! The girls in Clara's class didn't hesitate; they scattered, quivering with fear into the wings, leaving Maritza facing Clara in the middle of the stage.

Clara looked at her interestedly. She didn't feel the least bit frightened, knowing that the talisman would protect her. It was only when Maritza started to recite the words of a spell that Clara stiffened and took a step backwards. She knew it, Clara thought, suddenly horrified. Of course! How could she have been so stupid! She knew the spell that would draw the talisman to her! She'd memorized it from *The Book of Spells* before they'd stolen it! Maritza finished reciting the spell and with a triumphant scream of *"Eliandor!"* threw out her hands. To her horror, Clara felt the talisman loosen its grasp on her arm and fly in a gleaming, shining arc, through the air towards Maritza's greedy, grasping hand.

It was then that the Wind Witches dropped like stones from the flies, screeching like banshees. Manoeuvering her broomstick deftly, Wanda caught the talisman in mid-flight and held it aloft for all to see. "The talisman is mine!" she called out in the language of the witches.

Maritza, however, was having none of it. Nor was
she going to give it up that easily. Crouching down,
she gathered her strength and, propelling herself
violently upwards, leaped all of ten feet into the air
as Wanda passed, knocking the astonished witch
off her broomstick. With a jarring thud that made
the audience wince in sympathy, they hit the stage
together in a messy tangle of hats, cloaks and the
odd flash of striped stocking. Then, as the rest of the
Wind Witches soared and swooped overhead, still
screeching loudly, a totally unseemly scuffle ensued.

Samantha looked on disgustedly and, raising a
disparaging eyebrow at such uncouth behaviour,
dropped from the heights with her witches behind
her, ready to seize any opportunity that came her
way.

And, as it happened, she didn't have long to wait
... for Wanda and Maritza were so desperate to get
their hands on the talisman that they broke every
rule in the book — and when, at one stage, Wanda
suddenly let out a blood-curdling yell that made
everyone's blood freeze it was quickly accompanied
by another as she promptly bit Maritza back. No
one dared intervene as they kicked, jabbed and did
their best to pull one another's hair out. The end,
however, was unexpectedly swift. Maritza, gasping
for breath, staggered to her feet, drew back her
fist and delivered a punishing right to the chin
that would have felled an elephant. Wanda, not
surprisingly, crumpled at this devastating blow
and collapsed in a heap.

Grasping the talisman, Maritza ran to wings to
escape and to her horror, found the Snow Witches

waiting for her. Hovering on their broomsticks, she knew at a glance that there was no way she was going to get past them. Without breaking her stride, she swerved like a greyhound, ran back across the stage and, robes flapping wildly, headed for the battlements of the castle.

She's going to jump, thought Neil, as Maritza poised dramatically for a second before launching herself into space. However, even as she leapt for the safety of the mats below, the Queen of the Snow Witches, who had swooped across the stage after her, stretched out her hand and grabbed the talisman. The Snow Witches screamed in triumph as Samantha held it aloft and then turned in surprise as another, truly terrible shriek pierced the air; a shriek that held a variety of conflicting emotions — surprise, disbelief, unrelieved fury and much, much, more. It was terrible in its intensity and, indeed, to the discerning ear, had a resonance all of its own ...

Neil burst out laughing. He couldn't help it. Now he knew what the third form had been up to. They'd replaced the pile of gym mats with the biggest trampoline the gym had to offer! Maritza had, quite literally, got her come-uppance at last!

It wasn't only the audience who howled with laughter as Maritza bounced ever higher above the battlements. Samantha, still clutching the talisman, couldn't believe her eyes at first — but when she saw Maritza's startled, agonized face popping up again and again, she let out a joyful wail of unrestrained mirth and gleefully threw a hex so that Maritza continued to soar skywards.

Indeed, every time Maritza appeared, a furious, gesticulating jumble of black skirts and striped stockings, everyone creased up anew. Tears of laughter spilled down Neil's face as she bounced up time and time again; sometimes the right way up — often upside down — and always shrieking with rage.

The Snow Witches, helpless with laughter, were soon staggering round the stage, holding one another up hysterically. The Wind Witches, too, were every bit as bad. Wanda, of course, was still out cold but the rest of them were doubled up, clutching at their broomsticks as they howled with unholy glee.

Clara, however, didn't feel the least like laughing. She felt dreadful; she'd lost the talisman and, totally devastated, was set on recovering it. Ignoring the hapless Maritza and the helpless witches, she repeated the words of the spell. If Maritza could use it to take the talisman then she could use it to get it back again! It was as she said *"Simaron Eliandor"*, the final words of the spell, that the talisman left Samantha's hand and curved across the stage towards her.

Samantha, however, felt it leave her hand. Quick as a flash, she followed it on her broomstick and grabbed at it at much the same time as Clara. As they struggled, Clara knew instinctively that she was no match for the powerful witch. She needed help badly but as she looked round desperately, all she could see were witches and more witches.

Perhaps it was the sight of the black paper bats waving on their strings above the towers and turrets of the castle that spurred her imagination; perhaps the talisman was trying to protect her as it had when she'd fallen into the river or maybe *The Book of Spells,* itself, had a hand in the affair.

Whatever it was, the words of a spell flowed like running water from Clara's lips and as her voice rang out, clear and concise, in the ancient language of old magic, Samantha stepped back; white-faced, frightened and totally appalled.

22. Daemons

If Neil looked apprehensive at what was happening, his reaction was nothing to that of those on stage. They all knew from Clara's words that it was an ancient spell and gazed at her in disbelief.

Maritza stopped bouncing, the witches stopped laughing and with one accord, each and every one of them swung round to gape at Clara in horror. The old man, standing at the side of the auditorium stiffened in shock and drew in his breath with a gasp. Like the witches, he'd never heard the spell before but had more than a vague idea where it must have come from and paled at the thought.

Von Grozny, too, had been totally stunned at Clara's ringing tones and leapt from his seat to look warily at the old man who was swearing viciously under his breath. That they both felt the same was obvious and despite their enmity, an uneasy alliance was born. They both knew this was something the witches couldn't handle on their own.

"Come on, Vassili," the old man snapped, gripping his arm. "We're in this together. The little fool has no idea what she's done!"

Vassili, who had long since guessed the identity of the old man, smiled wryly. "Milord," he bowed,

"I am at your service."

And with that, two sets of cold, blue eyes, determined and desperate, gazed at the stage where a moving darkness heralded the arrival of the daemons of the spell.

Neil's heart sank as he looked along the row and saw them move purposefully towards the flight of steps that led up onto the stage. Their faces were those of soldiers going into battle against a mighty opponent and he gulped and wondered what on earth it was that Clara had conjured up.

He didn't have long to wait.

Glancing around, he saw that the entire audience was now totally engrossed in the action of what they blissfully thought was the plot and as his eyes moved again to the stage where the witches cowered in terror, a fearful shadow gathered itself in sweeping waves, like the folds of an enormous cloak, round the soaring turret of the castle.

Then they appeared, slithering from its slit windows in a never-ending stream, sliding softly from its darkness on outspread wings; dreadful creatures, the stuff of nightmares. Daemons! Winged creatures with the sleek heads of cats and the scaly bodies, feet and tails of lizards. Neil drew in his breath and the audience cringed as the fearsome creatures glided down on jagged, leathery wings. Red eyes gleaming and wicked-looking teeth curved menacingly over furry chins, they swooped across the stage with eerie, whistling cries, to attack the witches.

Clara took a couple of steps backwards, appalled at what she'd done.

"Daemons!" Samantha ground out as she lifted her arm to throw a hex.

Many of the witches were caught in the initial attack for, as the bats swooped from the tower, they landed on their backs, and crouching horribly, sank their teeth deep into the back of their necks. Total bedlam then erupted; the witches screeched in agony, hexes crackled through the air and disgusting clouds of black smoke rose from the stage as daemons went pop all over the place. A scene from hell couldn't look much worse thought Clara, staring in alarm at the devastation,

The audience looked on, wide-eyed and fearful. Even the staff sat up, looking more than slightly worried. It all looked so ... so real ... and, indeed, given the bedlam on stage, it could safely be said that any resemblance to a respectable school concert had long since flown out the window.

Maritza, hexing dacmons furiously, yelled across the stage at Samantha. "Make — her — get — rid — of — them!"

Clara heard her and looked at Samantha blankly, realizing that she hadn't a clue how to reverse the spell. "I can't," she said, looking at Samantha hopelessly. "I ... I don't know how!"

Samantha, also hexing daemons furiously, glanced at her in disgust. "Say the spell backwards, you fool!" she hissed.

Clara ran the spell through in her mind. Her thoughts were in turmoil and she had to think carefully to get the words in the right order. What, she thought, was the last word? Her mind raced through the spell and she said it aloud. Now the second last ...

It was then that she noticed Herr von Grozny and the old man darting among the witches, throwing crackling hexes at the daemons that leapt and swooped around them. Who was he? The confusion distracted her and, with her mind in free fall, she knew she had to get a grip. Taking a deep breath, she closed her eyes firmly so that she could concentrate on getting the words of the spell in the right order.

Heart in his mouth, Neil watched as, with the arrival of the old man and von Grozny, the pitched battle grew in intensity. Their hexes, he noticed, were much more effective than those of the witches and as the startled daemons started to disappear with alarming swiftness, their leader, perched dramatically on the battlements against the backdrop of the night sky, changed his tactics. At their master's command, the daemons immediately turned from the witches who, more than grateful to be thus ignored, promptly took advantage of this unexpected respite to disappear in a shimmer of light.

Red-eyed and evil, the cat-faced creatures folded their scaly wings and, crawling together, gathered in hunched, tight-knit bunches to concentrate their attentions on the two magicians.

As the Wind Witches disappeared, only the Snow Witches were left, staggering around looking totally exhausted. The battle, however, was by no means over and although Samantha hadn't a clue as to who the magicians were, she knew she couldn't move out; not until Clara had finished saying the words of the spell. She looked at her in exasperation, knowing that the whole spell had to be repeated backwards for the daemons to disappear. Eyes shut tight and concentrating hard, Clara, however, was oblivious to what was going on around her.

Samantha's lips tightened. Telling her to get a move on would only break her concentration and cause more delay but she knew perfectly well that if the child didn't hurry up, the magicians would soon be dead for both were in deep trouble, fighting desperately for their lives. Indeed, she wouldn't be surprised if the old man hadn't lost the battle altogether. She watched as, totally outnumbered, he struggled to fend off the daemons and as his eyes met hers, cried out in agony. "Samantha, get out of here and take Clara with you!"

Samantha looked dumbfounded. It couldn't be him, she thought wildly. How could it be him? She stepped forward sharply but was a second too late; he'd disappeared, pinned down under a crawling pile of scaly bodies and leathery wings.

It was then that Clara spoke the final word of the spell.

In an instant, the surprised daemons disappeared in a crack of sound and as the rippling cloud of darkness that swirled round the stage gradually faded to nothing, Samantha, too, muttered a spell, grabbed Clara round the waist and promptly vanished, taking her witches with her.

Gasping for breath, Maritza ran to the side of the stage and pressed the button that released the curtain. As it swung down she leant exhaustedly against the wall and thought at a rate of knots as the roar of applause from the other side of the curtain reached her ears. Another hex floated through the theatre and as Clara's class found itself assembling beside her with no memory of what had happened, she forced a delighted smile, lined them all up hastily, told them they'd been fabulous and took them in front of the curtain to take their bows.

The headmaster then made a speech of appreciation, remarking dryly and with some justification, that he'd never before seen such an exciting concert. Maritza, nodding and smiling at the side of the stage, agreed with him and bringing her forward, he stepped back and started to clap. So it was that with a twitch of her skirt and a tantalizing glimpse of striped stocking, Maritza took her bow to roar upon roar of delighted applause.

With all eyes concentrated on Maritza, Neil thought it a good time to disappear. Switching his magic ring to his left hand, he vanished unobtrusively and looked round. No one, he reckoned, had noticed that he'd gone and no one would miss him. Classes had finished for the day and all he had to do was wait until his form had filed out of the theatre. As rumours from the kitchen had been drifting round the Senior School all day, this happened remarkably quickly for everyone was anxious to get their helping of pumpkin pie and nobody hung around.

Even as the last class filed out, Neil was halfway

up the flight of steps that led onto the stage. He'd
seen the old man fall down covered in daemons
and had heard what he'd said to the Queen of the
Snow Witches. Had Clara been quick enough to
save him, though?

Creeping behind the curtain, he reached the
wings and looked onto the stage. Apart from Herr
von Grozny who was leaning over the old man's
body, it was completely empty. Thank goodness,
Neil thought, maybe *this* time I'll be able to find
out who he is. Walking very quietly, he could see
the concern on von Grozny's face as he treated the
old man's wounds. Funny, he thought, fleetingly,
his mind winging back to the night they'd faced
one another up in the library, I could have sworn
they were enemies.

"You'll be all right," von Grozny was saying
reassuringly. "I think I've neutralized the poison.
You'll be up and about in minutes."

The old man smiled weakly. "Thanks, Vassili,"
he whispered. "I owe you ..."

Von Grozny looked serious. "Will you tell me
how you come to be ... like this?" He lifted one of
the magician's thin, withered hands and looked at
him questioningly.

The old man closed his eyes, his lips twisting in a
sour smile. "I call it Malfior's Curse," he whispered.

"Malfior?" Vassili looked and sounded startled.

"Another story," the old man breathed, feeling
slightly better now that the pain was easing. His
eyes had been closed as he spoke and he missed the
look of complete surprise that had crossed Vassili's
face.

Neil didn't miss it, however, and his eyes sharpened as he watched the wolf man interestedly. Malfior! His attention was well and truly caught at the mention of the name, his mind immediately sweeping back to the previous year when he'd been involved with the Cri'achan, the great giants of the Highlands. How on earth did von Grozny know of Malfior?

"It was a spell," the magician continued, raising himself on one elbow, the colour coming back into his face, "an ageing spell that has nearly run its course." His wrinkled lips twisted. "I doubt if I have very much longer to live."

Footsteps suddenly sounded in the wings and as Neil swung round, he glimpsed Maritza, still in her witch's costume, heading towards them. By the time she reached the stage, however, it was empty. The two magicians had vanished.

Neil, however, was still there, his mind racing frantically. He barely noticed her for, just before the old man disappeared, he had seen beyond the lines of age.

Recognition had dawned and with it came shock, horror and disbelief. He knew *now* who the old man was.

23. Ice palace

Samantha sat back on the rose-coloured cushions and velvet drapes of her high, glittering throne of sparkling ice and triumphantly stroked the silver talisman that clasped her wrist. Her jet black eyes gleamed in the flare of the torches as she savoured the fruits of victory. She could hardly believe it. The talisman was hers at last. Its power, she knew, was breathtaking and as she pondered what she might do with it, her mind wandered from the prisoner who stood in front of her, to more pleasant things.

The prisoner was, of course, Clara, and as the queen's attention strayed, Clara looked discreetly round the Great Hall of her palace, wondering how on earth she was going to escape. It wouldn't be easy, she knew, but she definitely had a chance for although Samantha had immediately wrested the talisman forcefully from her grasp she hadn't taken her firestone and, more importantly, didn't seem to have noticed her magic ring.

Now she stood, waiting to hear what the queen had to say as the Snow Witches, once more dressed in their elaborate gowns of shredded chiffon, crowded around her, casting evil, venomous looks in her direction, whispering angrily amongst themselves. Many of their friends had been seriously injured as a result of her spell and they couldn't understand why Samantha hadn't finished this human child off the minute they'd got back. Clara shivered, she was pretty sure that had the queen not been there, they would have hexed her ages ago.

Ignoring the witches as best she could, Clara glanced round covertly, trying to memorize the layout of the ice palace in case she managed to escape. There were too many witches around at the moment, she decided, but maybe when there were just a few, she could use her ring. Once invisible, she could hide somewhere until Neil arrived with reinforcements. Her spirits rose at the thought. He was probably on his way to Arthur's Seat right now, she reckoned.

Looking around, she saw that the palace was remarkably light and bright. As well as the flaring torches that glowed from sconces in the walls, the vast room shone with a weird, unearthly blue glow that seemed to come from within the ice itself. High walls of carved ice rose to a ceiling of fretted domes; ice statues stood in niches round the walls; ornate arches gave a glimpse of pillared corridors and, dotted here and there throughout the length and breadth of the hall, were seating arrangements of delicately carved ice-furniture that decorated a floor as smooth as glass.

Clara shifted on her feet, shivering as the cold penetrated the soles of her shoes and the thin stuff of her costume. The movement brought Samantha back from her wonderful dreams of power and glory. She straightened and looked icily down on the fool of a child who had caused so much trouble.

Well, she wouldn't be around long enough to cause any more harm, that was for sure.

A snow witch entered through one of the delicately carved arches and bowed low to the queen. "If it please you, your majesty, you are needed," her voice was concerned. "There are so many wounded ..."

The queen rose to her feet, her face mirroring her anger. Clara wilted under the look of fury in her eyes and knew that the witch would have hexed her there and then had it not been for the old man. The question again hovered in her mind. Who *was* he? How did he know her?

The queen waved her hand angrily at Clara. "Imprison her, Matilda," she snarled, "in the deepest dungeon you can find!"

One of the Snow Witches rose importantly to her feet and moved forward. Like all the Snow Witches, she was incredibly beautiful, the plaited ribbons of her headdress framing a face spoiled only by the protruding pieces of black stone that were her eyes. She grasped Clara's arm, none too gently. "Bow to the queen," she instructed, twisting her arm behind her to make sure she obeyed.

Clara gasped in pain as the witch forced her to bow.

"We hope you enjoy your stay with us," Samantha remarked evilly, as she made to leave. The rest of the witches smiled at this and looked at one another knowingly; leaving Clara to wonder exactly what was in store for her.

"This way," Matilda ordered brusquely, leading

her through a high, curved arch that led into a long corridor of pillars interspersed with panels of gloriously fretted trellis-work. Idly, Clara wondered who had made the palace and all its wonderful decorations. Somehow she couldn't imagine the elegant, beautiful witches carving out the ice into all those fantastic shapes and designs. Maybe they'd used magic, she thought.

The witch kept a firm grip on her arm as she marched her down a sweeping staircase of ice steps and along yet another corridor, giving her no chance to use her magic ring. Whenever she stops to unlock the door to my cell, Clara thought, I'll use it then.

They walked on and Clara soon noticed that the further they went from the Great Hall, the more ordinary the decoration became. Gone now were the delicate arches and swirling curves of pillars and pediments. They'd reached a part of the palace that was no more than a low-roofed tunnel cut through roughly hewn blocks of ice. There were no doors anywhere and Clara was just wondering where they were going to imprison her when Matilda gave her a vicious push in the back that sent her hurtling forward.

She screamed and, as her scream echoed and re-echoed throughout the palace, Matilda smiled sourly. That'd teach her to interfere in the affairs of witches. Turning swiftly from the hole in the floor, she walked quickly back the way she had come. It wasn't a part of the palace that she liked and the sooner she was back in the Great Hall, the better.

The hefty push had been totally unexpected but it, in itself, wasn't what had made Clara scream. She hadn't noticed the hidden hole in the ice and when she found herself falling, she'd been taken completely by surprise. No wonder she'd yelled. Now she found herself sliding down a kind of snow-chute and her heart sank as she realized that it was going to be very, very difficult to escape from such a prison.

She landed in a slither of snow in what was not much more than an oblong-shaped chamber of ice. It glowed with the same cold, blue light that illuminated the rest of the palace and, looking round, she saw that apart from a tatty-looking old blanket that lay on a raised shelf of ice, there was nothing else in the room.

She sat down feeling scared and hopeless. How long were they going to keep her in this awful prison?

24. Rescue plans

"The magician that hexed Clara, it ... it was Prince Kalman," Neil said, later that evening when he arrived, cold and tired inside Arthur's Seat on an exhausted broomstick. He was still amazed at his discovery. "I heard the wolf man talking to him ... Herr von Grozny," he whispered, looking from the MacArthur to Lord Rothlan and Lady Ellan, "and Prince Kalman said he was dying ..."

There was a long silence. Kitor and Cassia, who had flown beside Neil on his journey north, looked frightened. Both had, at one time, belonged to the prince and he hadn't treated them with kindness. Amgarad, too, squawked and flapped his wings strongly from his perch on the back of Lord Rothlan's chair. The prince had never been one of his favourite people, either. He had spent years locked in the body of a monstrous bird as a result of Kalman's scheming. It was no surprise that he loathed him. Even Arthur, the great dragon, didn't seem unduly upset at the news of Kalman's plight. His death would be no great loss to the world of magic. He blew a cloud of smoke down his long nose and then looked apologetic as Archie and Hamish started to cough. The sight of the sparkling smoke, however, reminded the MacArthur of his pipe and, fishing out his favourite briar, he avoided his daughter's stern gaze and started to fill it with tobacco.

Although the MacArthur had looked thoughtful and glanced at Lord Rothlan when he heard Neil's words, he hadn't seemed particularly surprised. It was Archie, Hamish and Jaikie who'd sat up in amazement, every bit as startled as Neil had expected.

"You knew, didn't you?" Neil said suddenly, looking accusingly at the MacArthur. "You *knew* that the old man was the prince!"

"Actually, *I* told him," Lord Rothlan confessed, with an uneasy smile. "I saw Hughie a few months back when I was visiting the Lords of the North in Morven and ... well, he told me that Kalman was ageing fast and that he was afraid he was going to die. Hughie and Kalman always got on together, you know."

Neil's eyes dropped. Hughie, whose cottage lay on the slopes of the mountain, was a great guy and he'd never been able to understand how he could like someone as nasty and arrogant as the prince. He shrugged. "The other thing Prince Kalman talked about was Malfior," he continued, meeting Lord Rothlan's gaze. "He said it was Malfior's fault that he was dying." Jaikie and Hamish looked at one another with raised eyebrows as Neil finished slowly. "He called it Malfior's Curse."

Again there was silence and Neil looked round in surprise. There was obviously something going on that he didn't know about and it didn't look as though they were going to tell him, either. He flushed, feeling angry and embarrassed. They'd never kept anything from him before and it was more than a bit hurtful. Knowing that they must have a reason, however, he kept his voice level. "What about Prince Casimir?" he asked. "I mean, does he know? Can't he do anything to help him?"

"Prince Casimir is with the Sultan in Turkey," the MacArthur said. "He knows nothing of his son's condition and we haven't told him."

"You haven't told him?" Neil's voice rose incredulously. "But ... but he's his father! It's his right to know!"

"It's like this, Neil," Lord Rothlan sighed, "before he left Morven, Kalman made Hughie swear that he wouldn't tell anyone, especially his father, what was happening to him."

"So Kalman's going to let himself die rather than go to his own father?" Neil looked incredulous. "That's just ... plain stupid!"

"The truth is, we just don't know what to do about Kalman," the MacArthur admitted. "He and his father ... well, it's what you might call a difficult relationship."

"If he'd ask us for help, we'd give it," Lady Ellan sighed, "but you know how arrogant he is, Neil — and if we were to offer it, I think he would reject it."

"He's too proud for his own good, that's his trouble," Neil said in exasperation. "You weren't in Hughie's cottage when he told us about going into the Halls of the Giants and the yellow light that shone from Cri'achan Mor's eyes. Malfior's Curse, he called it. It took his magic power from him."

"And left him with something evil ..." the MacArthur mused. "But why ..."

Lord Rothlan's eyes sharpened at his words. "That's a point," he nodded, "and yet there was no reason for Malfior to single him out, was there? I mean ..." he shook his head, his brain sifting through a variety of possibilities.

"Maybe there's more to this than meets the eye," the MacArthur said, making a great palaver of lighting his pipe and then drawing deeply until it started to belch out clouds of foul-smelling smoke.

"What I'd really like to know is why you didn't tell us that the magician was Prince Kalman?" queried Neil. "Why didn't you?" he repeated, looking serious and more than slightly offended. "Prince Kalman, of all people! He hates us, you *know* he does. And he could have hexed us or anything. He was inside the school. I thought he was the janitor."

"But he *didn't* hex you, did he?" the MacArthur pointed out. "On the contrary, he made sure that you escaped from von Grozny in the library."

"Yes, well ... but ..." Neil stopped and frowned. The MacArthur was right. He *had* saved them from von Grozny. He looked little short of flabbergasted. The very thought of Prince Kalman saving them from harm was so novel that he couldn't quite take it in.

"You said that he told the Queen of the Snow Witches to take care of Clara, too," Lady Ellan said quickly.

"Well, not take care of her exactly," Neil frowned,

trying to remember the shouted words, "but Samantha grabbed her before they all disappeared. Clara *and* the talisman," he added.

The MacArthur sighed. "I'll be honest with you, Neil," he said, adjusting his cushions until he was comfortable. "The reason we didn't tell you that Kalman was the old man was that we knew he wanted the talisman himself. As long as he didn't have it, we knew he would keep you safe from the witches and von Grozny."

"But he didn't," Neil pointed out shortly. "The witches nearly hexed me in the Black Bull and *he* hexed Clara when she was in the middle of the river. If she hadn't been wearing the talisman, he'd have taken it."

"In that case, I think he must be more desperate than we thought," Lady Ellan said, frowning.

"And when he told the Queen of the Snow Witches to take Clara with her, I don't think he had her safety in mind!" added an aggrieved Neil.

"Oh, I think he did," Lord Rothlan objected. "Kalman has a lot of influence with the Snow Witches and very little with the Wind Witches or the Earth Witches. He wouldn't want Wanda or Maritza to capture Clara; that's why he deliberately gave her into Samantha's care. Despite what happened on the stage, she won't dare harm Clara, you can be sure of that. He's still a powerful magician."

As this very thought had been worrying Neil all the way north from the Borders, his spirits rose as he followed Rothlan's reasoning. "So what's the next step?" he asked. "How do we get Clara back?"

Again there was a silence and Neil felt his heart sink. Surely they weren't going to leave Clara with the Snow Witches ...

The MacArthur puffed at his pipe, Lady Ellan looked thoughtful and Archie, Hamish and Jaikie eyed one another sideways and said nothing.

"We'll need Arthur's help, I think," Lord Rothlan said, looking up at the dragon. "Are you game for a battle or two, Arthur?"

Everybody cringed as he said this as they knew what Arthur's answer would be. It was as they'd expected. Arthur, beaming at the thought of action, blew a delighted stream of glittering smoke down his long nose. Enveloped in its clouds, everyone started coughing, spluttering and waving their hands.

"For goodness sake, put your pipe out, father," Lady Ellan snapped. "Really, between the pair of you, I don't know which of you is the worst!"

As the smoke faded, Lord Rothlan smiled reassuringly at Neil. "Jarishan is built from solid stone and Arthur very nearly captured it, didn't he, my dear?" he said, turning to his wife as he spoke. Lady Ellan raised her eyebrows with a smile as she remembered the days when they had been enemies. She nodded and he added. "Samantha's palace isn't nearly strong enough to stand up to a dragon and knowing her as I do, I can assure you that she won't be prepared to see it melt around her ears."

By this time, everyone was tense with excitement at the thought of an attack on the Snow Witches' palace.

"We'll leave at midnight, I think," the MacArthur looked at Arthur enquiringly. "We can't afford to waste any time."

Archie, Hamish and Jaikie rose purposefully to their feet. If they were leaving in a few hours time then there was work to be done.

"You can stay here and keep Neil company, m'dear," the MacArthur said calmly. "We oughtn't to be away for long."

Lord Rothlan paused and looked at his wife with a wry smile.

Lady Ellan got to her feet and gave her father a look that would have sunk a fleet of battleships. *"Stay and keep Neil company!"* she snapped, her voice rising by more than a couple of octaves. "You must be out of your mind, father." She looked across at Neil and smiled. "We're going too, aren't we, Neil?"

He grinned and nodded appreciatively. Lady Ellan on her high horse was quite something!

"Nothing," she added, smiling with deceptive sweetness, "would keep me away! After all, I have quite a few old scores to settle with dear Samantha."

25. Snow worms

Clara lifted her head and looked round. There it was again; a strange, scrunchy noise. But where was it coming from? She looked at the roof of her cell and the opening of the long tunnel that slanted upwards to the witches' palace but could see nothing. She'd have tried to climb it if she could but it was too high for her to reach. Otherwise it would have been an easy job to chip away at the ice, make footholds for herself and climb out. Escape was so near and so far away!

After she'd dusted herself down and shed all the clinging ice particles that she'd gathered on her way down the long chute, she'd sat on the mouldy-looking old blanket cross-legged and hugged herself tightly to keep warm. It was so boring. Time passed ever so slowly and once again she wished she had her watch on. Maritza had told them before the play that witches didn't wear watches so she'd left hers in her room. If only she'd put it in the pocket of her costume, instead. It was awful, not knowing what time it was. She seemed to have been here forever already; a couple of hours could have passed or even more, she couldn't tell.

She closed her eyes and tried to work out where Neil would be by this time. She was pinning her hopes on him. Surely he'd have reached Arthur's Seat by now and told the MacArthur what had happened? Then they'd come to rescue her. The thought brightened her spirits and gave her hope for a few minutes but as the cold reality of the ice-dungeon penetrated her limbs, she rubbed her hands and her arms to keep warm.

Then she heard it again. The scrunchy, scratching noise. Whatever was it? Knowing that it was far too soon for the MacArthurs to have come to her rescue, she got to her feet and walked round her prison. The noise seemed to come from the wall opposite her bench. Gingerly she put her ear to the ice and heard it quite clearly. It was coming from inside the wall. Someone was coming to rescue her!

She banged on the ice with her fist. "I'm here!" she shouted. "I'm here! Help me!"

The scrunching noise stopped for a long moment and then she heard it start up again, coming nearer and nearer. Excitedly, she sat back on the blanket and waited, eyes bright at the thought of being rescued.

Then the noise sounded again, but this time it seemed to come from behind her. She turned round and put her ear to the wall. Yes, someone was trying to reach her from the other side, as well.

Then she saw it ... a long, snake-like shape in the ice. A shadow of alarm crossed her face as she pushed her hair behind her ears with nervous fingers and backed away. What on earth was it? She'd imagined some kind of machine, drilling its way towards her but this thing was alive and moving, coming closer and closer through the ice.

It was now so close that she could see its black eyes looking at her as it ate its way through the wall of her cell.

She screamed as it broke the ice; a horrible, huge, worm-like thing, at least four or five inches across with a rounded head, greedy black eyes and a gaping mouth that seemed to have as many teeth as a great white shark. It was pushing its way into the room and she knew she had to stop it. But how? She had nothing to defend herself with. Except her shoes, that is. Desperately, she pulled one off. She'd always hated them. Good, solid, school shoes built to last for yonks! Well, at least they'd come in handy now!

Holding it by the front, she lifted it up and brought the heavy heel down on the worm's head with all the force she could muster. The worm, not unnaturally, objected to being bashed on the head and promptly started pulling itself back into the ice, leaving behind a scatter of broken teeth on the floor of the cell. By this time, Clara was shaking with relief but when she heard a crackling noise behind her, swung round in alarm. She'd forgotten about the other one! Rushing towards it, she hammered it back into the ice the minute it stuck its head through the hole, sharp teeth gnashing ferociously. Snow worms, she thought, eating their way through the ice. Were they responsible for the many decorations in the snow queen's palace — the pillars, the statues and the fragile furniture?

She looked round. The worms had disappeared and there were no other threatening shadows in the ice. The danger seemed to be over — for the present, at least. She sat down on the bench of ice, breathing heavily. The thought of spreading the blanket over it and trying to sleep to pass the time until Neil came to rescue her had crossed her mind, but now she didn't dare shut her eyes in case the worms came back.

They did come back. She heard them before she saw them. Indeed, her ears had been straining to catch the first sound of their approach and she listened fearfully as the noise grew steadily louder as they ate their way through the ice. But what, she thought, if it wasn't only ice they ate? What if *that* was what the witches had known? Did they know the worms would kill her in this small, cold cell in the ice? Was that to be her punishment for calling up daemons?

And the spells she had learned were less than useless for, without the talisman, she was no longer able to call up any of the dreadful residents that lurked in *The Book of Spells* — even if she'd wanted to, which she didn't! But she shivered in fear as the noise of the worms grew increasingly louder and gritted her teeth desperately. There wasn't a lot she could do, which was a pity as she was quite sure they were coming to kill her. The teeth on them, she thought hopelessly, would make short work of an elephant far less someone her size.

The noise was coming from everywhere this time: she could see vague shadowy shapes in all four walls. Hurriedly, she took off both her shoes and held them ready to fend off her attackers. Her feet soon felt like lumps of ice as the cold seeped through the soles of her cotton socks. Come soon,

Neil she thought frantically. There are so many of them and I won't be able to hold them off for ever.

She could see them quite clearly now, writhing and slithering in the walls, their great teeth slicing quickly and easily through the ice. How many were there and which one of them was going to poke its head through first?

The worms, however, had a game plan. They had learned their lesson well and after the failure of their first attempt, were wary. This time, they took it in turns to poke their heads just a little way into the cell before withdrawing them quickly. Then, two more made the same manoeuvre on opposite walls and at the same time, so that she had to swing round to thump them. They were too quick for her, though, and she missed the pair of them.

The worms kept the attack going for what seemed an endless length of time and Clara felt her strength waning as she was kept continuously on the move. Gasping for breath and with a stitch in her side she stood in the middle of the cell and watched through tear-stained eyes as the worms, sensing triumph, pushed further and further through the holes they'd made. It only needed one, she thought, to get through completely and she'd be finished. While she was trying to kill it, the others would slide through and they'd finish her off.

"Help!" she screamed at the top of her voice. "Help me! Please, help me!"

But even as she screamed, a huge, long, thick worm slithered swiftly from its hole, dropped into the cell and, slavering jaws agape, headed straight for her.

26. Wolf man

"Majesty," a Snow Witch moved hurriedly between rows of ice shelves that held the bodies of injured witches. "Majesty, we have visitors," she said excitedly as she bowed low. "The two magicians that helped us against the daemons; they're here!"

Samantha straightened, her face strained. "I can't come now, Matilda. They'll have to wait," she said tiredly. "The daemons' poison is deadly and even the healing power of the talisman takes time to work. I've still a long way to go before I finish treating everyone."

"Majesty," Matilda looked doubtful, "they need help themselves. The old man is ill."

"My witches must come first," Samantha said icily. "The magicians will have to wait. See that they're comfortable and I'll come as quickly as I can."

Matilda bowed and withdrew. The talisman that shone on the queen's arm had filled the court with a new sense of power and importance. She was going to enjoy telling the magicians that they would have to wait.

It was very much later that Samantha sailed majestically into the Great Hall. Approaching the magicians regally, she apologized profusely

for keeping them waiting. Words, after all, cost
nothing and although it was only a small show
of her new status, she knew it would not go
unremarked. It was only when she met the icy,
blue eyes of the younger of the two men that her
heart quailed and she understood why her witches
had grouped themselves as far away from her
guests as possible without seeming rude. A wolf
man! One of the Onegin!

The wolf man bowed, but not, she noticed, too
low. "Count Vassili Onegin," he said coldly, clicking
his heels, "special envoy of Lord Jezail of Ashgar."

The queen's eyes flashed venom at Matilda, who
paled visibly, knowing that the queen's punishment
would be severe. "You are welcome, milord, and
you have my sincere apologies," she said. "I was
not told who my guests were otherwise I would
have come immediately. Please forgive me."

He inclined his head and indicated the old man
who lay with his eyes closed on one of the spindly
ice sofas. "Prince Kalman was badly bitten by the
daemons and although I've done my best, he seems
to have need of more help than I can give."

Bending over the prince, a ripple of unease
trickled through her as she felt the count's eyes
staring fixedly at the talisman clasped firmly round
her arm. She wasn't a fool and knew perfectly well
that the envoy of Lord Jezail had surely come with
but one thought in mind — to take the talisman
back to his master in Ashgar.

Half an hour later, the queen, accompanied
by her ladies in waiting, ushered her guests to a
private sitting room where tea was being served.

Prince Kalman had regained consciousness and no longer looked so desperately ill; the pallor had left his face and although still fragile, he walked with a firm step. What, Samantha wondered, had happened to leave him in such a state? He'd obviously fallen victim to a spell of some sort and a very powerful one at that. Gone was the fair-haired, debonair young prince that she knew — he looked, she thought disdainfully, at least a thousand years old, if not more.

Prince Kalman brought the subject up himself. Finishing his tea, he put the cup and saucer on the table and looked at Samantha with more confidence in his tired, watery eyes than he felt. He knew from past experience that witches were a tricky lot and bore watching. "Count Vassili brought me here, Samantha," he began, "so that I could ask a favour from you; a very great favour."

"Indeed," she answered warily.

"We have been friends for many years, you and I," he said, forcing a smile, "and as you see I have been affected by a powerful spell. It is a spell that is slowly taking my life, as you may have noticed."

Politeness forced her to speak. "How can I help?" she asked, half-guessing the answer as she spoke.

"By letting me wear the talisman until the spell is destroyed," he replied. "Its magic is powerful and I know that my time is near."

Samantha's face darkened. "Give you the talisman!" she repeated with an incredulous laugh. "Do you think I've lost my senses?"

"I need it, Samantha!" Kalman's face flushed.

"You know as well as I do that it has the power to cure spells. I wouldn't ask for it otherwise."

Again she laughed derisively. "Do you take me for a fool, Prince Kalman?" she snapped. "Your father and the Lords of the North have the power to counteract any spell that binds you. *You* know that just as well as *I* do! Ask *them* for help and don't come to me with fairy tales!"

"You know I can't ask my father," he replied stiffly, "and the Lords of the North have barred me from Morven. What I say is the truth!"

"And *I* don't believe you," she countered. "What madness! If I were to give you the talisman, I'd never see it again!"

Kalman's face whitened and the count half-rose to calm him down.

Samantha, too, got to her feet and looked at them fiercely. "Understand this," she said harshly. "The talisman is mine and I give it to no one. Not to you, Prince Kalman, nor," and here she glanced at the count, "to you or your master, Lord Jezail."

"I will convey your message to my master," the count said smoothly, rising to his feet.

Prince Kalman, too, stood up, his face stony with anger and despair. Then he remembered Clara. "Where is the child?" he asked, looking round. "Didn't you bring her with you?"

"I did," Samantha answered and, knowing how deeply he hated the two children, smiled to soften his disappointment at not getting the talisman. "Don't worry," she said sweetly, "I've taken care of her. She'll trouble you no more."

Kalman stiffened and looked at her in alarm.

"What exactly do you mean by that?" he asked sharply.

"She's in the deep dungeons," came the casual answer.

"You mean you've put her among the snow worms?" he sounded incredulous.

"Ages ago," she smiled. "They ought to have finished her off by this time."

The count leapt forward and grabbed the prince's arm as he lunged furiously at the queen.

"You fool!" Kalman gasped, struggling frantically, as he tried to reach her. "You complete fool! Do you think the Lords of the North will stand by and do nothing? If she's dead you'll suffer for it, Samantha — talisman or no talisman!"

"I couldn't care less!" she snarled, rising to her feet. "She was mine to punish by right!" She threw out her arms in anger. "Do you know how many of my witches the daemons injured," she hissed, "how many lie poisoned by their bites?"

"Where is she?" Kalman demanded in a voice that brooked no denial.

"Find her yourself," the queen spat. Then she stepped back, white with fear. The witches standing at her side screamed shrilly and at their cries, more poured in from the Great Hall. They stopped dead in their tracks, however, as they looked towards the queen; for the Ashgari count had disappeared in a shimmer of light and in his place stood a great, grey wolf.

The wolf bared its teeth threateningly and growled at the petrified witches. Then, nudging Prince Kalman with its head, looked up at him.

"Follow me," the wolf said, "I know her scent." And it ran from the room, sniffing the ice.

Kalman gave the queen one last, furious look and followed. The wolf ran to the area around the queen's throne and started to sniff the ice, searching for Clara's scent.

"This way," he said, and trotting steadily so that the prince could keep up with him, made his way along corridors and down a flight of stairs until they came to the roughly carved tunnel where the dungeons were. It was then that they heard Clara's scream of pure terror and the noise of a struggle as she hit out frantically at the snow worms with the heels of her shoes.

27. An unexpected rescue

As Clara's screams echoed eerily from the depths of her prison cell, the wolf circled the hole in the floor undecidedly but the prince, knowing the ferocity of the snow worms, unhesitatingly threw himself into it, feet first. He shot down the chute and, landing with a thump, quite successfully flattened the rearing snow worm that was threatening Clara.

Clara, pressed fearfully against the wall of her cell, looked at the old man in startled wonder, recognizing him immediately. The school janitor, she thought in utter amazement. What on earth was he doing here? She wasn't quite sure if his arrival improved the situation or not.

The snow worms, however, had no such doubts. They knew a magician when they smelt one and, backing swiftly into their holes in the ice, slithered swiftly off. Clara watched them go and relaxed, her legs trembling under her as shock set in.

"Sit down, Clara," the old man said, kicking the dead snow worm to one side. "You've had a bad fright but it's all over now. The snow worms won't come back."

"They might," Clara observed, her voice shaking. "They looked hungry and there are two of us now."

Kalman almost smiled. "Ah, but I'm not a prisoner,"

he said. "I've come to get you out of here."

Hope flared in Clara's heart but her eyes were puzzled as she looked at him. "Who *are* you?" she asked. "I don't know you but ... but you seem to know me." Then she met his eyes and stiffened in fear. Recognition was instantaneous. "Prince Kalman?" she whispered fearfully, shrinking backwards.

He bowed abruptly and then glanced at the shoes she still held in her hands. "Better put those on," he said shortly and turning to look up at the entrance to the chute called out. "Vassili," he shouted. "Vassili, are you there?"

There was no answer.

He called again, but there was silence.

"Vassili?" Clara repeated, hardly able to believe her ears. "You mean Herr von Grozny is here *as well?*"

The prince looked suddenly tired. "He *was* here," he said. "I hope he's gone to find a rope but I might well be mistaken."

Clara looked at him in sudden understanding. "Of course," she muttered, "*he's* after the talisman as well, isn't he?"

The prince nodded, his lips pressed together in disappointment. "It's my fault. I should have known better than to trust him."

It was then that Clara realized that her feet really were freezing. Bending down, she took off her sopping wet socks and used the end of the long, black skirt she'd worn for the play, to dry her feet before pushing them awkwardly into the heavy leather shoes.

"I hope the daemons didn't injure you very badly," Clara asked, seeing the lines of pain on the prince's face. "I'm really sorry," she apologized, tying her shoe laces firmly. "I should never have cast that spell."

"No, you shouldn't!" he agreed sitting up straight and looking at her coldly. "Where the devil did you get it from?"

"From *The Book of Spells*," she answered.

He looked at her very oddly indeed. *"The Book of Spells,"* he repeated slowly, his eyes widening incredulously. "Er ... do, please go on," he said, waving a hand invitingly. "Don't stop there! May I ask where you stumbled upon this ... this treasure ..."

"I don't think it's a treasure exactly," Clara said slowly. "There are a lot of good spells in it, of course, but there are awful spells, too."

"So I gathered," the prince said dryly. "Like conjuring up daemons!"

Clara looked shamefaced. "To tell you the truth, I really wish we'd never stolen it," she muttered.

"May I ask who you stole it from?" Kalman regarded her coldly but with a tinge of grudging admiration in his glance.

"The Earth Witches," she confessed.

"So *that's* what you were up to that night," he said, looking startled. "If I'd known you were carrying *The Book of Spells* I might well have behaved differently."

"You were there?" she looked at him in astonishment. "At Witches' Wood? I don't believe you!"

He froze her with a look of contempt. "I don't

lie," he said, "and you have cause to be grateful to me, you know. You left a trail of footprints across that field that would have put the witches right on your trail."

"*You* helped us?" she looked at him directly, still unable to think of him as the prince. "Why would you do that?"

"I didn't want the witches to catch you," he said simply. "I wanted the talisman myself."

Clara looked at him seriously. "Why? Haven't you enough power?"

His lips twisted in a wry smile. "Not enough to cure the spell that is killing me," he said.

Clara blushed. "I ... I'm sorry," she muttered, feeling dreadful.

He rose to his feet and walked slowly up and down. "I told you," he reminded her. "It was when I was in the Great Hall of the Giants," he muttered. "Malfior hexed me."

"I thought it was Cri'achan Mor," Clara looked at him in surprise.

"Malfior was looking at me through Cri'achan Mor's eyes," returned the prince.

"But Malfior died," Clara frowned. "And," she added, "so did Cri'achan Mor. Wouldn't their spells have died with them? Isn't that the rule?"

The old man stopped and nodded slowly.

"Then it must have been someone else who hexed you," Clara pointed out reasonably, "someone who had merged with Cri'achan Mor, perhaps."

Kalman smiled sourly. "Forget it," he advised. "Only a great magician could get close enough to Cri'achan Mor to be able to merge with him and

I don't believe that any of the Lords of the North would punish me in this way."

"There are other magicians," she pointed out, looking worriedly at the shambling figure. "There's the Sultan in Turkey although I'm sure he would never hex you like this."

"I don't believe that either," he admitted.

"Then what other magicians do you know?"

"Well, some in China and a few in India but I never heard of any of them travelling so far from home ..."

"What about Lord Jezail?" enquired Clara.

"Lord Jezail?" the prince looked at her and shook his head with a thin smile. "No, Jezail would never hex me like that. Why, my father and I have known him for years. We used to stay with him in the citadel at Stara Zargana when we were on our way to Turkey to buy magic carpets. He's a friend of the family. Besides which, he hasn't been in Scotland for years."

"Oh, but he has," Clara looked at him in surprise. "When Neil and I were in Morven last year I heard Lord Rothlan and the MacArthur talking about Lord Jezail and the giants."

"Are you sure?" Prince Kalman frowned.

"Positive," Clara said. "I wasn't eavesdropping, you know," she added, anxious that he shouldn't get the wrong impression, "I just happened to hear a bit of their conversation when I was passing. Of course, I'd never heard of him then."

"Jezail?" the prince repeated, shaking his head doubtfully. "I can't believe it!"

"He was with the giants," she said firmly. "I heard

them say so." Clara's eyes, clear and honest, met his quite openly and he could not but believe her.

"So Jezail was there all the time," he muttered, his face darkening as realization dawned. "He was there all the time," he repeated, "in the halls of the giants. *He* hexed me!"

"Are you all right, Prince Kalman?" Clara asked anxiously as he suddenly swayed on his feet, groped for the bench and toppled forwards. "Prince Kalman!" she shook his shoulder and fear curled inside her as there was no response. His body was sprawled half on and half off the bench and with an effort she managed to lift him onto it and pull the blanket under him so that at least he wasn't lying on ice.

The prince looked dreadful, she thought, but, thank goodness, he was still breathing.

It was then that she thought of using her firestone to help him. But would one be enough to have any effect? Mind you, the MacArthur had loaded hers with extra magic and that might make a difference. She unfastened the chain that held her firestone and lifting the old man's head, for she couldn't think of him as Prince Kalman, she looped it round his neck, fastened it and pushed the firestone under his shirt.

The results weren't instantaneous but after a while she noticed that his breathing had eased and later, when she was walking up and down, flapping her arms about to keep warm, she saw him move. He rolled over onto his side and with relief she realized that he wasn't unconscious any more. He was asleep.

Again she looked up at the entrance to the chute. "Herr von Grozny!" she called. There was no answer and she turned despondently away. Why did nobody come? Where were Neil and the MacArthurs? Surely they should have come to rescue her by this time?

28. Dragonfire

The ice palace of the Snow Witches was breathtaking. It reared high, slender and majestic from a plain of barren ice. Neil had never, in his life, seen anything so fragile or so beautiful. High ice walls, battlements and soaring towers glittered in the sun. The Earth Witches' castle under the copse in Witches' Wood was nothing in comparison.

"They've seen us," Lord Rothlan said, flying alongside Neil on his carpet. "Look, they're closing the great gates." Neil looked across the smooth, white expanse that stretched between them and the castle and saw white figures pulling at silver doors, heaving them shut. Snowmen, thought Neil, just like the ones they'd seen on the moors.

As their carpets skimmed high above the surface of the ice, Neil looked back in wonder at the huge army of MacArthurs that Jaikie and Hamish had so efficiently organized. Store cupboards deep under the hill had been opened and although armour and weapons had been quickly distributed, it all took much longer than an anxious Neil had expected. Clara, he knew, would be relying on him to come to the rescue and by this time, he reckoned, she'd be worried stiff and wondering what on earth had happened.

He had to admit, however, that the extra time had been well worth it as the entire army, resplendent in shining armour flew impressively towards the castle on hundreds of magic carpets. Pennants in gold, red and black, showing a dragon rampant, fluttered bravely from spears and lances held at the ready and as they neared the castle, archers reached over their shoulders to fit arrows in their bows from quivers slung across their shoulders.

The witches, clustered fearfully on the battlements, watched the approaching army in horrified wonder. The sight of the MacArthur's troops was bad enough but what really scared them was the enormous dragon that flew threateningly above the ranks of the soldiers on their flying carpets. They had heard tales of the great dragon that lived in Arthur's Seat but this was the first time they'd seen him and they hissed and screamed in alarm as Arthur suddenly sent a blazing stream of sparkling fire through the air.

"Summon the ice men," ordered the queen, "and let them give battle!" Trumpets sounded and as the array of magic carpets approached, a great crack of sound announced the arrival of the ice men. Neil gaped, for they lifted from the plain itself; jagged of limb and armoured in ice they rose in their thousands; strange, helmeted creatures carrying sharp, slender spears. Volley after volley of the thin, razor-sharp spears glittered as they curved through the air in relentless waves towards the MacArthur's troops who raised their shields against them. The spears were then followed by clouds of arrows from the archers on the battlements.

It was the dragon, however, that was worrying the queen. She had little protection against such a fearsome creature and a lot less power than she'd had minutes previously — for the wolf man had returned alone from the dungeons and wrested the precious talisman from her arm in a snarling fury. She hadn't been able to resist and although she'd thrown the most powerful hexes she knew when he had appeared snarling at the door, she had been unable to harm him. His protective shield was such that her hexes didn't even bounce, they died, dropping in pitiful bursts of colour to the floor as he'd stood there, all powerful and demanding. Then, leaping across the floor in great bounds he had changed once more into a man. The struggle that followed was brief and his fingers, still half wolf claws, had pulled the talisman from her arm. His eyes, blue, cold and empty met hers for a few seconds before he vanished in a shimmer of light.

It was then that Matilda had rushed in with the news of the approaching army.

"Majesty," she cried, trembling with fear, "they come in their thousands and — and majesty, they come with a dragon!"

Samantha paled and, straightening her headdress and torn gown, strode swiftly along corridors and up endless flights of stairs until, at last, she reached the battlements. Matilda, she thought sourly, as she took stock of the situation, might have over-estimated the size of the approaching army but she hadn't underestimated the size of the dragon. It was huge!

Now she watched in helpless fury as Arthur, with

Archie on his back, swooped over her beautiful towers and turrets and sent long breaths of sparkling fire swirling round them. The towers immediately started to melt and the screams and cries of horror from her witches drifted out across the plain of ice.

It was over in minutes, for Lord Rothlan had been right. Samantha surrendered immediately. She couldn't bear to see her beautiful palace melt round her ears and as she knew she was going to lose the battle in the end she would, she decided, rather lose with her palace in one piece than be left standing in its ruins.

"Well, Samantha?" the MacArthur said, shifting uncomfortably on one of the spindly chairs that decorated the Great Hall, hoping that it wouldn't collapse under his weight. Lord Rothlan, too, had eyed the furniture distrustfully at first but it was proving stronger than he'd given it credit for.

Samantha looked a wreck of her former self. Her robes were torn, her hair tangled and her face lined with exhaustion. She gave a gesture of defeat. "If it's the talisman you want, then I'm afraid I must disappoint you. I don't have it."

Neil looked at Lord Rothlan. "Who has it, then?" Rothlan asked, addressing the queen. "Clara?"

Samantha looked positively terrified for a moment. "No," she said, shaking her head. "The wolf man took it," and as she rubbed her arm they could see where the wolf's claws had left two red, bleeding weals.

There was a deathly silence. "And Clara?" asked the MacArthur in a voice of steel. "Where is she?"

29. Harsh punishment

Lord Rothlan and the MacArthur looked at one another in growing alarm as the queen, scrunching her ivory robes with nervous fingers, continued to mouth soundless words. Her witches, too, looked petrified and watching her, Lady Ellan felt her heart sink as a feeling of acute fear gripped her. Indeed, she was just about to rise from her chair and physically shake the words out of the trembling queen when the dreadful silence was broken by a calm voice from the doorway.

"Majesty," Matilda said, "I have brought the child and the prince as you commanded. Shall I bring them in?"

Everyone, except Samantha, who would have fallen over had she attempted anything so energetic, leapt to their feet and stared beyond Matilda to the two wet, bedraggled figures that stood framed in the delicate fretwork of the arched doorway.

Clara and Prince Kalman!

Lady Ellan gave a cry of distress as her eyes fell on the prince. Eyes wide, she shook her head in horror, trying to see in him the slim, fair-haired, handsome young man that she remembered. It was impossible. This old man was surely a stranger.

As everyone turned towards Clara and the

prince, Samantha met Matilda's eyes with a look
of such relief in them that Matilda almost preened
herself; for the look of heartfelt gratitude in the
queen's eyes was all that she had hoped for and
more. She straightened proudly and the frightened
Snow Witches, cowering beside the throne were
quick to note her new status. Once again in the
queen's favour, her position was assured.

Lady Ellan's cry, however, had brought Hamish
and Jaikie running into the room, followed by a
host of armed MacArthurs who approached in full
armour, spears at the ready.

Samantha, now totally petrified, slumped back
in her chair, shuddering violently as reaction set
in. Hiding her trembling hands under the chiffon
folds of her gown she could hardly believe what
had happened. How the child had managed to
survive, she didn't know, but thank goodness
she had, or the MacArthur's army would have
destroyed her and razed her beautiful palace to
the ground.

Clara came slowly into the hall, her arm
supporting the weak, shambling figure of the
prince. She smiled shakily as she looked round.

Neil ran towards her, his face reflecting his
anxiety. It had been a mistake to delay their
departure for so long, he thought. They should
have left Arthur's Seat at once! Clara looked a
complete mess, her face white and cold and the thin
black material of her witch costume no protection
whatsoever against the freezing temperature of
the Snow Witches' palace. "Clara," he asked, "are
you okay?"

"Yes, but I'm freezing," she said, shivering. "Honestly," her voice was aggrieved, "I thought you were *never* coming!"

Lady Ellan swept up behind Neil and, taking off her cloak, wrapped it round Clara's shoulders, muttering a hex as she did so. "This'll warm you up, Clara," she said, hugging her.

"The prince ..." Clara protested, tightening her grasp on the prince's arm as he tottered unsteadily on his feet. She knew from his eyes that he was on the verge of fainting again, for the effort of getting out of the cell had used up the little energy he'd had left.

"Clara ..." he muttered, desperately, "I can't ... can't ..."

At that moment, Lord Rothlan strode up and, nodding at Clara to let go, put a strong arm round the prince. "You're quite safe now, Kalman," he said gently. "We'll look after you."

Kalman looked into his eyes and a smile twisted his lips. "Thanks, Alasdair," he whispered. Then his eyes closed and he passed out.

Looking round, Lord Rothlan gestured urgently to Jaikie and Hamish to help him support the prince. The MacArthur, too, came forward, looking concerned.

"He's in a bad way," Lord Rothlan said briefly, looking at Kalman's pale face. "We have to get him to Morven at once."

The Macarthur nodded and clapping his hands together sharply, called one of the magic carpets.

"We'll have to use your carpet," he said apologetically to Neil. "I hope you don't mind?"

Neil shook his head. His only thought was for the prince who looked unbelievably old and frail.

"You and Clara will have to travel back to Edinburgh with Archie. Arthur will be able to carry the three of you quite easily," he said rapidly, "but we've got to get the prince to Morven as quickly as we can. It's only the Lords of the North who can save him now."

Neil nodded. He was, of course, concerned for the prince but at the mention of the dragon, his insides had started to churn with excitement. To travel on Arthur's back all the way to Edinburgh ...! His eyes shone at the thought.

Hugging Lady Ellan's cloak round her, Clara watched in relief as the magic carpet sailed up and, at the MacArthur's command, hovered beside them. Jaikie and Hamish helped lift the prince's frail body onto the carpet, while Lord Rothlan slipped his cloak from his shoulders and wrapped it carefully round the still figure.

"I'm going with him, Jaikie," he said. "The carpet can carry us both."

Jaikie and Hamish nodded. "Safe journey," the MacArthur said briefly. "We'll keep in touch with you through the crystal once we've sorted out this little lot!"

"What about Herr von Grozny?" Clara asked suddenly, looking puzzled. "Is he still here?"

"Von Grozny?" Lord Rothlan asked, his head jerking in surprise. "You mean, von Grozny was here, too?"

Clara nodded. "He came with Prince Kalman. They saved me from the snow worms."

"Snow worms!" Lord Rothlan repeated in a terrible voice, turning to look disbelievingly at the queen.

Samantha, who had hoped that the snow worms would never be mentioned, turned as white as a sheet and cowered in her chair. She shot a wild glance at Clara. "What did you expect me to do with her?" she cried defensively, her voice shrill with fear. "She called up daemons against my witches ..."

The MacArthur looked grim but it was Lady Ellan who moved determinedly forward. "I'll deal with this, father," she said quickly. "You see the prince on his way and I'll settle with *dear* Samantha."

The MacArthur nodded briefly and after exchanging a few hurried words with Lord Rothlan, watched as his carpet rose into the air and, floating through one of the delicately carved, arched windows that lined one wall of the Great Hall, disappeared from view.

Lady Ellan, in the meantime, narrowed her eyes as she surveyed the snow queen who, huddling apprehensively on her throne, wondered what dreadful fate lay in store for her.

Given Lady Ellan's fury, she soon found out.

"You may not know it, Samantha," Lady Ellan began in a deceptively honeyed voice that held distinct undertones of steel, "but I possess some ... quite remarkable powers."

"You do?" the queen quavered.

"Yes," Lady Ellan continued, "I ... er, have the ability to see into the future."

"You ... you have?"

"Shall I tell you what I see in the future, Samantha?" she asked gently.

The queen nodded, looking at Lady Ellan with awful fascination.

"I see that the winter in Scotland this year is going to be very mild," she said blandly, *"very* mild, Samantha!"

Samantha looked devastated as the implication hit home.

"M ... mild?" she whispered, appalled.

"Remarkably so," Lady Ellan repeated in a voice of iron. "In fact," she observed, "it will be *so* mild that not one single flake of snow will fall. Not one, Samantha! Do you understand?"

Samantha nodded, looking as though she were going to burst into tears at any minute.

"Not one, anywhere, over the whole of Scotland!" Lady Ellan made her message quite clear.

"Not ... one?"

Lady Ellan shook her head.

The queen's shrill cry of anguish rose high above the keening wails of her witches. Such a dreadful punishment was unheard of. Pressing her hands to her face in horror, she watched disbelievingly as the MacArthur, nodding in approval, put an arm round his daughter.

"And," he added, for good measure, "if anything were to happen to either Clara or Neil in the future because of you — well, let's just say that your Snow Witches would be looking for a new queen very shortly afterwards! We would all make sure of that!"

Samantha, now totally demoralized, nodded dumbly and hid her face in her hands.

The MacArthur met his daughter's eyes approvingly. "I think we can go now," he said. "Where's Archie? I've told Neil that he and Clara can join him on Arthur's back."

Seeing that everyone was preparing to leave, Clara started forward anxiously, catching at the MacArthur's cloak. *"But what about Herr von Grozny?"* she asked anxiously. "I mean, where is he?" She looked questioningly at Matilda. "You were there," she said accusingly. "What happened to him?"

Matilda, who had moved towards the throne to console her devastated mistress, looked round at her words and came towards them. She curtseyed briefly. "I was on my way to the battlements, Miss, when the wolf man appeared and," she looked apologetically at her mistress, "forced me to help him. I think he wanted to make sure that the prince was still alive before he left, for when he pulled him up out of the cell, he told me to ... to look after him well." She paused and shrugged slightly at her liberal translation of the threats the count had made should anything nasty happen to the prince before help arrived. "Then he cast a hex and disappeared," she said softly. "He is long gone."

"With the talisman?" Clara asked, although she already knew the answer to the question.

Matilda nodded. "Yes, Miss," she said slowly, "with the talisman."

"I see," Clara said, lowering her eyes so that no

one would guess the sense of loss that enveloped her. The talisman had gone. It was no longer hers! And she missed it! Aware that Matilda was looking at her strangely, she smiled somewhat ruefully. "Well, anyway," she said, "thanks for pulling me out of the dungeon."

"The wolf man commanded me," Matilda answered, giving the queen a sidelong glance to make sure she was listening. "I could not refuse."

With that, she curtseyed again and as the little group bowed to the queen and left the hall, she turned to her shivering mistress with a sigh, murmuring soothing words. It was going to be a long, hard winter for them all, she mused.

Not one, single, solitary flake of snow!

Not one!

A severe punishment, indeed.

30. Homeward bound

"There's Edinburgh," Neil said suddenly, pointing eastwards as the dragon lost height and altered course slightly.

"It won't be long now," Archie said, turning his head so that they could hear him against the rush of the wind. "I can see Arthur's Seat already!"

Clara's heart sank at Archie's words. She was enjoying the flight so much that she didn't want it to end. Hugging Lady Ellan's cloak about her, she looked beyond the dragon's horned head to the sprawling carpet of lights that pierced the total blackness of the night. Edinburgh! The wonderful journey would soon be over. She patted Arthur absent-mindedly. There was nothing quite as wonderful, she thought, as flying through the air on the back of a dragon. She'd flown on Arthur before, of course, but this had been a really long flight and she'd enjoyed every single minute of it, fascinated by the movement of the dragon's steadily beating wings as he powered them through the air at tremendous speed.

Part of her mind, however, was still with Prince Kalman; although she still found it difficult to think of him as the tottering, frail old man who had rescued her from the snow worms. She wondered, too, if Lady Ellan had reached Morven; for once she'd dealt with the Queen of the Snow Witches, she had summoned her carpet and after a hurried word with the MacArthur, had left to follow her husband to the magic mountain that housed the blue and silver halls of the Lords of the North, the powerful magicians who ruled the world of magic.

She knew that they would do everything they could to save Prince Kalman's life, but could they, she wondered. He'd looked so frail when Lord Rothlan had helped him onto the magic carpet. Thank goodness she'd given him her firestone, she thought. It had made a difference and at least given him the strength to climb out of the ice cell. And as she idly wondered why Herr von Grozny had passed the rope to Matilda and hadn't waited to see her safe, a cloud of unhappiness settled over her. The talisman had been left to her and although she missed it, her feelings were mingled with a growing sense of unease at the trouble it had caused. Maybe, she thought finally, it was just as well that Herr von Grozny had taken it back to his master in Ashgar.

She was suddenly jerked back to the present as Arthur's wings tilted sideways as he again changed course and lost some more height. Neil looked down as the lights beneath brightened and became clearer. It was almost over, he thought, trying to save the wonder of the flight in his memory. It had been so exciting and just a pity that they hadn't been able to fly closer to the ground as only tiny pin-points of light had marked the presence of the many towns and villages that they'd flown over on their way back.

What was even more fascinating was the fact that he knew they weren't alone in the sky. Although he couldn't see them, he was well aware that a horde of magic carpets flew in serried ranks behind the dragon; for the MacArthur and his army, too, were heading for home and would be glad to see the lights of Edinburgh looming on the horizon.

"Hang on, Clara," Neil cautioned, clutching Archie tightly, "I think Arthur's going to do his disappearing act into the hill again!"

In this, he was quite correct, for although Arthur was losing height, he was also picking up speed and as the rush of wind increased, Clara buried her head in the rough wool of her brother's cloak and shut her eyes. This was the bit she hated. It had happened before when they'd been on Arthur's back, escaping from the giants in the Highlands. Arthur had flown straight into the side of the mountain and although they'd passed through it without feeling a thing, it was dead scary nevertheless.

"You can open your eyes now," Archie announced. "We're through!"

Clara gave a sigh of relief and straightened as the familiar, tapestry hung halls of the MacArthur loomed before her eyes. Arthur's great wings had stopped beating and now stretched silently as he glided down to the raised dais where the MacArthur's carved, wooden throne stood in all its grandeur.

Archie slipped off Arthur's back with the ease of long practice and turned to give Neil and Clara a helping hand as the dragon held out one of his wings so that they could clamber easily to the ground. Turning his great head to see that they were okay, he looked at them fondly, his wonderful eyes glowing. Neil ran up and threw his arms round the dragon's neck. "Arthur," he said, "that was totally fab! Wasn't it, Clara?"

"Absolutely brilliant!" she agreed.

Arthur took a deep breath and although Archie, Clara and Neil knew what was going to happen, they didn't have the heart to say anything as he roared out a stream of blazing fire that curled upwards in a breathtaking shower of dancing sparks. It was great to be back, he thought. He'd had a wonderful adventure and although he would have enjoyed melting the Snow Witches' palace round their ears, well ... you couldn't have everything, he supposed. His eyes shone with happiness. Everything had gone well, no one had been hurt, they'd saved Prince Kalman and he'd had Archie, Neil and Clara for company on the flight home.

The inside of the hill was warm and welcoming and as Neil and Clara looked round, they could see the magic carpets emerging from the tunnels that opened onto the cavern. It was a fantastic sight as wave after wave of carpets soared in, landed their occupants here and there all over the cavern floor before drifting off to sheltered alcoves where they rolled themselves up tiredly and settled to a well-deserved rest.

Jaikie and Hamish waved as their carpets landed but immediately turned to the task of sorting out armour and weapons from the returning troops. The MacArthur, however, seeing Clara's pale face, muttered the words of a hex. She needed to eat before she returned to school. They both did.

"Food," thought Clara, as the smell of roast chicken drifted round her heart. Now that she had time to think about it, she realized that she was really starving. The MacArthur gestured them both forward and, pulling out the chairs that were drawn up round a little table, gestured to them to be seated. Clara sat down gratefully and tucked her chair in, delighted to be once again in safe, familiar surroundings. Thoughts of the snow worms, the witches and the talisman started to fade from her mind as the MacArthur heaped slices of roast chicken on her plate and served her with vegetables. It had been some adventure, she thought, but it was over now. She smiled across at Neil who, eating hungrily, still had no idea of what she'd gone through. There would be plenty of time to talk over what had happened, she thought. There was no hurry. It would all come out later.

31. Talking things over

When they'd finished eating, the MacArthur looked at them thoughtfully. "You'll have to double up on Clara's magic carpet," he said, remembering that Neil's had been used to take Prince Kalman to Morven. "It ought to be able to carry the pair of you quite easily."

"Do you think anyone at school will have noticed that we're not around?" Neil asked. It was a thought that had been worrying him as he knew perfectly well that if they were missed, the school would have phoned their parents. And that spelled major trouble!

The MacArthur shook his head. "When you arrived here and told me what happened at the end of the concert — when Samantha took Clara — I put a memory spell on the school. No one will have missed you and, from what you've told me, the carpet will be able to take you straight into your bedrooms without anyone noticing."

Arthur, still excited from his adventure, was blowing fire everywhere, but, seeing that Neil and Clara had finished their meal and that Archie, Hamish and Jaikie had joined the MacArthur, he calmed down and made his way to the dais, where he curled up comfortably beside them. Kitor and Cassia also flew over, settled their feathers and prepared to listen to Neil and Clara's latest adventure.

"Before you go back to school, Clara, we'd like you to tell us what happened when Samantha took you back to her palace," the MacArthur said. "Start at the beginning and take your time. Don't miss anything out."

Clara drew her cloak around her and began. "Well," she said, "when the Queen of the Snow Witches hexed us all off the stage and we arrived at her palace, the witches were really nasty to me. And I can understand why," she added. "They were still suffering from the shock of the daemons' attack — and so was I," she admitted, "although I tried to hide it. The queen had taken the talisman, of course, and was wearing it. She was using it to cure her witches. Anyway, she was busy and had no time for me so she told Matilda to put me in a cell in the ice ... and the snow worms found me."

The MacArthur's face darkened and Arthur, who hadn't heard that part of her story before, hissed in anger. He wished now that he *had* melted her palace to the ground!

"I kept them off as best I could but I only had my shoes to bash them with. If I'd had the talisman," she said reflectively, "I might have been able to use a hex from *The Book of Spells* but when I thought about it, it didn't really make much difference, for daemons would've been every bit as bad as the snow worms, if not worse."

Neil glanced at her, feeling more than slighty ashamed of the thoughts that had crossed his mind for he'd been secretly rather glad that Herr von Grozny had taken the talisman. He hadn't been jealous, exactly, but had felt a bit left out of things when Auntie Muriel had left it to her. Not that he'd grudged her it but still ... he was glad that it had gone.

"Anyway," Clara continued, "it was when one of the snow worms managed to get into the cell that Prince Kalman arrived. Actually, he landed right on top of it. Totally flattened it," she said, with a half smile. "The rest of the snow worms disappeared and ... well, we sort of got talking. I said I was sorry for casting the daemon spell and he asked where I'd got it from. So I told him. And, do you know, Neil, he was there when we escaped from Witches' Wood? He said we'd left a line of footprints across the field that would have put the witches on our trail."

Neil looked horrified. "I never thought of that," he admitted.

"He told me he rubbed them out because he didn't want the witches to find the talisman. He wanted it for himself so that he could use it to cure himself of Malfior's spell. And then I said that as Malfior and Cri'achan Mor were both dead, how could it be their spell?"

The MacArthur's head jerked sharply as she said this and his eyes narrowed shrewdly. So where had the hex come from? His mind started to race.

"Bravo, Clara," Archie said softly.

"Anyway, we worked out that the spell must have been cast by a magician that had merged with Cri'achan Mor and the only one I could think of that would do such a thing was Lord Jezail. Prince Kalman wouldn't believe me at first, but you see," she looked at the MacArthur, "I'd overheard you and Lord Rothlan talking about Lord Jezail when we were in Morven and when I told him that he'd been in Scotland at the time, he got a real shock and ... and, well, that was when he sort of fainted."

The MacArthur nodded. "You're quite right, Clara," he admitted. "Lord Jezail was responsible for Malfior."

Neil frowned thoughtfully. "I've just remembered something that might be important," he said hesitantly.

"Go ahead, Neil," the MacArthur said, looking at the boy's serious face.

"It was after Clara disappeared with the witches," Neil began. "Do you remember me telling you that I went backstage to see if I could find out who the old man was?"

"And it was Prince Kalman," the MacArthur nodded.

"Well, Herr von Grozny was trying to help him. He was asking him how he had become so ill and old and ... and Prince Kalman muttered something about Malfior's curse. Von Grozny turned as white as a sheet at the mention of Malfior. The prince had his eyes shut and didn't notice a thing but von Grozny's face — I can't describe it. He looked ... absolutely devastated."

A puzzled silence followed this remark.

"Look, I'm not saying you're wrong, Neil," Jaikie frowned, "but what you've just said doesn't really add up, you know. Count Vassili is Jezail's right-hand man. He *must* have known of Malfior."

"He might have known of Malfior but he certainly didn't know about the hex Jezail put on the prince," Neil stated determinedly.

"I think Neil's right about that," Clara nodded, "After all, Herr von Grozny did his best to help Kalman, didn't he?"

"It still doesn't hang together,"Jaikie objected. "Prince Casimir and Prince Kalman were close friends of Lord Jezail. After all, they used to stop over in Ashgar on their way to Turkey, didn't they?"

The MacArthur nodded.

"Surely it'd take a lot more than a quarrel," Hamish objected. "He must have really *hated* Kalman to put such a *vicious* spell on him."

"I think Lord Jezail *is* vicious," Neil interrupted, "and quite frankly I don't believe for a minute that Prince Casimir stole the Sultan's Crown. If he did, I bet Lord Jezail *hexed* him to do it! I mean ... it could have been a hex ... couldn't it?" he said, sounding suddenly doubtful.

There was a surprised silence as everyone looked at one another, appalled at the implications of Neil's words.

"A hex ... to make Casimir steal the Sultan's crown, you mean?" Hamish looked amazed.

"A hex!" the MacArthur said in a completely different tone of voice as though Neil's words confirmed a long held suspicion. "Do you know, I believe you're right, Neil! That would explain so many things! I've always thought there was something odd about Casimir stealing the crown."

"And maybe Kalman turning so ... so power-hungry," added Jaikie, sitting up straight in his excitement. This new angle on Lord Jezail opened up all sorts of possibilities! "But why," he wondered. "Why would he do such a thing?"

"He wants power," the MacArthur said immediately. "It can't be anything else. Jezail was always ambitious, you know. And he is a powerful magician in his own right. I rather think he wants to rival the Turkish Sultan. After all, the first thing he chose to steal was his crown."

"He didn't have the courage to steal it himself, though," Archie broke in excitedly. "He must have known that the Sultan would destroy him if he found out he'd taken it."

"So, as Neil says," the MacArthur continued, "he hexed Prince Casimir to take it, instead!"

"*And* take the blame if things went wrong," Hamish pointed out. "Which they did!"

There was a grim silence as they thought of the Sultan's punishment; for Prince Casimir had spent many years imprisoned in the desert as a result.

"Do you think Count Vassili knows all this?" Neil asked.

"I doubt it," the MacArthur shook his head. "Don't forget it happened years ago, long before he arrived in Jezail's court. Besides which," he added, "he's hardly the type."

"I agree," Clara said. "After all, when he took the talisman from the Queen of the Snow Witches he didn't just buzz off to Ashgar, did he? He came back with a rope to rescue us."

"Why didn't he take you out first?" queried Neil.

"Prince Kalman couldn't have got out on his own if I'd gone first," she explained. "I don't know if it was the daemons' bites or the shock of realizing that it was Lord Jezail who had hexed him, but, as I said, he'd collapsed. I'd already put my firestone round his neck to help him, like Lord Rothlan did with Amgarad when he was ill."

The MacArthur nodded approvingly.

"Anyway, when Herr von Grozny shouted down to me, I told him he'd have to take the prince first. I don't really think Kalman knew what he was doing. The rope had a loop at the end for him to put his foot in and I managed to get him to understand that he had to hold on. Then von Grozny hauled him up and the rope came down for me. But when I got out, it was only the snow witch that was there. Herr von Grozny had vanished." She pursed her lips and frowned slightly. "I think it was because you were attacking the castle," she mused. "After all, he knew you'd win and he wouldn't want you to capture him and take the talisman."

The MacArthur rose to his feet, looking serious. "You've done well, Clara," he said. "I'm sure you're right about Lord Jezail. And the more I think about it, Neil," he added, "the more I think you're right about the hex on Prince Casimir. The Lords of the North will certainly have to be told about all this."

32. Morven

If the little hobgoblin told his story once that day, he told it a thousand times, for he had been serving the Lords of the North with breakfast that morning when he'd noticed the strange magic carpet as it swept in through the blue and silver halls of Morven. His goat-like little face blazed with excitement and his slanted yellow eyes gleamed at the memory, as he told anyone who would listen how, the minute he'd seen the carpet, he'd called out a warning. After all, he pointed out reasonably, most visitors arriving in Morven came through the magic mirrors and were generally expected. They didn't arrive out of the blue in the early hours of the morning when it was still dark; and anyway, carpets that carried mysterious, crouching figures were unheard of. No, he'd known right away that something was up!

"I almost dropped a jug of orange juice," he confessed. "Well, I mean, I just froze! No one knew what to expect! After all, it could have been absolutely anybody or anything!"

The little group of hobgoblins nodded seriously knowing that the lords had taken notice of his shouted warning and risen hurriedly to their feet — but it was only when one of the figures on the carpet waved a greeting and a great eagle appeared, soaring in after the carpet, that everyone relaxed. It was Amgarad and his master, Lord Rothlan.

It was a dramatic arrival. The exhausted carpet stopped beside them, barely able to hover. It would be a long time, too, before Rothlan forgot the look of startled wonder on Lord Alarid's face as he pushed back his chair and hurried forward to help him off the carpet.

"Alasdair," he said anxiously, formality forgotten, "are you all right? What has been happening and who ..." he saw the cloaked figure of the old man lying unmoving on the carpet, "who is this?"

Lord Rothlan straightened himself with an effort, for he had cradled Kalman in his arms all the way to Morven. Stiff as he was, however, he managed to bow low as Lord Alarid and the other lords crowded round the hovering carpet. "It's Prince Kalman," he answered, pulling back the folds of his cloak so that they could all see the incredibly old, withered body that lay crumpled, still and barely breathing.

"Prince Kalman!" A whisper of sound rustled round the gorgeously robed figures as the lords looked at one another in amazement.

"He has been hexed by some evil thing," Lord Rothlan said harshly, "and I have brought him here, to Morven, to be cured."

He looked challengingly round the faces of the lords, waiting for one of them to point out that Prince Kalman had been barred from Morven for many years.

No one did, however. The sight of the prince had

given them all pause for thought and more than one of the lords looked guilty and ashamed. The tense silence was only broken when Lord Dorian, the prince's most severe critic, stepped forward. "We may have had our disagreements with Prince Kalman in the past," he said, with a slight quiver in his voice, "but I do not think that any of us wished him such harm." He paused. "Leave him as he is on the carpet, Alasdair. He must be cured at once. My lords," he looked round the gathering, "there is work to be done."

Lord Rothlan looked at him, feeling more than slightly stunned. Alasdair! he thought fleetingly. Never, for as long as he could remember, had Lord Dorian called him Alasdair. He must be more upset than he seemed. Nevertheless, his spirits rose. Action had been called for. They were going to do their utmost to save the prince.

"I can't believe it's Prince Kalman," Lord Alarid whispered, looking worriedly at the pitiful figure as they joined hands to form an unbroken circle round the carpet.

"He's wearing a firestone," Lord Dorian pointed out. "Shouldn't we remove it first?"

Rothlan frowned and pulling back the collar of the prince's shirt, quickly unfastened the thin gold chain that held the firestone. Clara's firestone, he was sure of it. Good girl, Clara, he thought, slipping it quickly into his pocket.

"Are we ready?" Lord Alarid questioned, looking round. "Then we'll use the Restoration Spell," he said, "at maximum strength."

In the background, the hobgoblins watched

in fascinated wonder as the circle of magicians chanted the words of the spell over and over again. Time passed and nothing seemed to happen and then the chanting slowed and stopped. The circle of hands was broken and a smiling Lord Alarid stepped forward to help Prince Kalman off the carpet.

And it was the Prince Kalman they remembered; tall, fair-haired and handsome even in the rags of clothes that the old man had been wearing. A quick hex changed this, however, and he laughed as he looked down at his new robes. So it was that, resplendent in his new finery, the prince stood before them, once more a Lord of the North.

Lady Ellan, who had followed her husband to Morven, had landed unnoticed except by Amgarad, who had flown towards her and perched on her shoulder as the magicians chanted the words of the spell. Now she moved swiftly forward to greet the prince and then stopped, looking in amazement from Kalman to her husband. "I can't believe it, Alasdair," she stammered looking at the prince in wonder. "It's not that you've just grown younger, Kalman," she smiled. "You look ... well, you look a different person."

At her words, everyone nodded in agreement for, as Lord Rothlan remarked later, he *was* different. He was looking at the Prince Kalman he had known as a boy, the Prince Kalman who had been, in times past, one of his best friends. The sneering, nasty, discontented individual of later years had vanished completely.

For the hobgoblins, it was the beginning of a

very exciting day as a succession of visitors started to arrive through the magic mirrors. First to appear was Prince Casimir, Kalman's father, who had been told nothing of his son's dreadful plight. He embraced him warmly, quite overcome with emotion and Kalman, too, cried unashamedly in his father's arms.

It was only once they had both recovered their composure that the Sultan approached and greeted the prince graciously enough, given the enmity there had been between them. Lord Rothlan then brought Hughie into the mountain and saw the pleasure and amazement in his face as he realized that the ageing spell had been lifted. Kalman was once more the young prince that he had known and liked.

Then the MacArthur appeared, called from Arthur Seat to greet Prince Kalman. To everyone's surprise he was followed by Neil and Clara who looked round the gathering shyly. It was all so ... so *very* grand.

Once the MacArthur had greeted the prince, Lord Alarid beckoned the children forward and it was as Neil approached to bow to the prince that he started to panic. What on earth was he going to say, he wondered. After all, he'd regarded the prince as an enemy from the first day they'd met.

"Well, Neil," Kalman said with a rueful twinkle in his eyes, "can you forgive me for the harm I've caused you in the past?"

Neil found himself smiling back, quickly realizing that this was a completely different person from the prince of old. His cold, arrogant manner had gone and the blue eyes that met his, were friendly and warm.

"And you, Clara?" the prince asked. "Lord Rothlan told me that without your firestone I might well have died on my way here," he said seriously.

Clara blushed. "It was nothing," she said.

"It meant a lot to me," Prince Kalman said quietly, "and I will never forget it."

Neil and Clara looked at one another and then back at the prince. Now that the hex had been lifted, they suddenly realized that they were going to like this new Prince Kalman very much indeed.

It was a time for celebration and the hobgoblins listened avidly as all the lords made speeches to welcome the prince back to Morven — even grumpy old Lord Dorian had been kind and when they had ushered the prince to take his place on the silver throne beside Lord Alarid, the prince had looked blazingly happy and proud.

The speeches were followed by a great banquet and it was only afterwards when everyone relaxed in comfortable armchairs that the MacArthur stood up, his face grave.

A ripple of unease ran round the assembled lords who looked at one another apprehensively, wondering what was coming next.

"I know you will all have noticed that I did not come alone," the MacArthur said, gesturing towards Neil and Clara, "but your invitation came at quite a startling moment."

"What happened, Father?" Lady Ellan enquired, her voice tinged with anxiety.

"When your invitation came, Clara had just finished telling me of Lord Jezail's part in this business. From what you said, Prince Kalman, she worked out that it was Lord Jezail who put the ageing spell on you. Not Malfior, as you had thought?"

The Prince nodded. "I couldn't believe it at first," he said, turning to his father who sat by his side. "I always thought he was our friend ..."

"Neil, however," the MacArthur continued, looking at father and son, "reckons that this wasn't the first spell that Lord Jezail cast. He thinks that he cast one many years ago when you were both on your way to Turkey to buy magic carpets."

A startled murmur ran round the assembled lords.

"Indeed," the MacArthur continued, knowing that he had everyone's undivided attention, "Neil thinks that Lord Jezail hexed you, Prince Casimir, to steal the Sultan's crown."

There was an angry gasp from the assembled lords.

"A hex!" Prince Casimir rose to his feet. "Of course!" he looked round wonderingly. "That must have been it! Why didn't I realize it before! A hex! It ..." he turned to the Sultan, "... milord, it explains everything!"

"I think he hexed you, too, Prince Kalman," Neil interrupted, "when he found that his plan to take the crown from your father had failed."

"And," Lord Rothlan interrupted thoughtfully, "if what Neil says is right, then I think, too, that he changed you into the terrible person you became; totally obsessed by the crown and the power it would give you."

The Sultan who had been listening closely to what was being said, now rose to his feet. Everyone followed suit and watched as he took Prince Kalman's hands in his. "I think that Neil and Clara are correct in what they say and I realize now that in the past I have accused you and your father unjustly and would ask your forgiveness."

There was an outburst of clapping and a buzz of conversation as everyone discussed what had happened. Lord Jezail's evil nature had finally come to light and it was a matter the lords were taking seriously.

Neil and Clara felt more than a bit embarrassed by the fuss that was made of them and it was only much later, when all the excitement had died down, that Lord Rothlan gave Clara back her firestone, Neil tucked his carpet under his arm as, with the MacArthur, they said goodbye to the Lords of the North.

Jaikie, Hamish and Archie were waiting for them when they stepped back into the hill through the magic mirror. Arthur, too, was delighted to see them back and blew a great burst of fire that sparkled brightly across the cavern.

"I don't want to hurry you," the MacArthur said with a smile, "but it's getting late and you really ought to be getting back to school."

"What time *is* it?" Clara queried, looking at her wrist before remembering that her watch was in school.

"Gosh! It's ten past six in the morning," Neil answered, looking at his watch.

The MacArthur nodded. "That's what I mean.

If you leave now, you might get back in time for breakfast," he added.

"That's true," Neil answered. "Thank goodness it's Friday. At least we have the weekend to look forward to."

Clara stared at Neil anxiously. "You've forgotten," she whispered. "The final performance of *Pumpkin Pie* is this afternoon. All the parents will be there! Mum and Dad are coming!"

Neil sat up. "Gosh! I'd forgotten all about that!" he muttered.

Seeing their horrified faces, Kitor and Cassia flapped their wings anxiously and looked at the MacArthur. "Don't worry about the school play," he said with a broad smile, "we'll make sure that it's a wonderful performance!"

And it was.

33. Moving on

"I *still* think the MacArthur should have told us," Mrs MacLean said angrily as they sat round the living room fire that evening. "I've never heard the like of it. Snow worms, indeed! They sound awful!"

"They were," agreed Clara, "but, I told you, Mum. Prince Kalman saved me."

"And he's a different person now that he's a Lord of the North," Neil reminded her. "I told you — really fab! You'll like him, Mum! We did!"

"If he saved you from these snow worms you keep talking about," her father interrupted, "then he *must* have changed for the better!"

"Well, actually, I don't think he had much of a choice," Neil said, considering the matter. "He'd know that the Lords of the North would be as mad as fire if they heard he'd let her be eaten by snow worms and done nothing about it."

"Don't say things like that, Neil," his mother scolded. "I still ..."

"... think the MacArthur should have told you," Neil repeated. "I know! I know! But look, Mum, can't you understand! There was no time! If they'd waited for you to get to Edinburgh from here, Clara *would* have been eaten by snow worms!"

"Honestly, I'm fine, Mum," Clara assured her yet again. "Now, can we change the subject, for goodness sake? How did you enjoy the play this afternoon?"

"Pumpkin Pie?" her father said, bursting out laughing at the very thought of it. "It was excellent! Really excellent! I've never seen such a good school concert."

"And serving slices of pumpkin pie afterwards was *such* a good idea," continued her mother. "It finished the afternoon off nicely. Really," she mused, "I'm so glad you're enjoying Netherfield. Muriel would be pleased to know you like it."

"And you played your part very well, Clara," added her father.

"Such a pity that the teacher who wrote it was ill, though," Mrs. MacLean said, looking at the clock on the mantelpiece and thinking vaguely about supper.

Neil and Clara looked at one another and grinned. They hadn't quite got round to telling their parents that Miss Markham was a witch, knowing that they would freak. The Headmaster had made polite excuses and covered up her absence fairly well but the fact that Miss Markham and Herr von Grozny had both disappeared at the same time had raised quite a few eyebrows among both staff and pupils. Rumours, needless to say, had raced round the school like wildfire but none of them were anywhere near as fantastic as the truth.

John MacLean looked at Clara seriously. "And you say that it was your German teacher, the wolf man, who got the talisman in the end?"

Clara frowned. "Yes, Dad," she said, "and to tell you the truth, I'm glad I don't have it any more. I know Auntie Murial did it for the best but I think she was wrong to have left it to me in the first place."

"*I'm* glad it's gone as well," her mother said, getting up to go to the kitchen. "I still can't believe the trouble it caused! The whole of the Borders was turned upside down what with the scarecrows, the snowmen and the witches. But I must say," she continued, "that it's been lovely actually living here. Your dad's done a bit of gardening and I've been finding my way round the shops in Berwick and Coldstream."

"Yes," her husband smiled, "now that the builders have finally finished, we can relax and enjoy our new house — at long last!"

There was a pause. Suddenly Edinburgh and the Royal Mile Primary seemed very far away.

Neil and Clara looked at one another. "I know," John MacLean admitted, "it's like living in another world down here, isn't it. I'll find it strange leaving Edinburgh after all these years as well."

"Has anyone moved into the cottage yet?" Clara asked, thinking back to their old house beside Arthur's Seat. "Have you been given a date yet?"

"Actually, I meant to tell you sooner," her mother answered. "Robbie Moffat's moving in next Monday. He's taking over your dad's job and he and his wife want to move in before the end of the month. You can understand it," she added. "They have young children and want to have everything sorted out before the Christmas rush begins."

"And I've been offered job as Estate Manager on one of the big estates down by the river, so it all fits in rather nicely," their father added. "They want me to start at the beginning of December."

"Gosh! Great, Dad!" Neil said, looking pleased. "That's fantastic!"

"Isn't it," Janet MacLean smiled happily. "Everything seems to be working out very nicely. And it looks as if you won't be boarders for much longer," she continued as her husband left the room to answer the telephone. "I must remember to pop in and see the school secretary next week to arrange places for you both on the school bus."

Clara's face brightened. Neil had made loads of friends at school but she hadn't really settled to being a boarder. The thought of taking the school bus backwards and forwards was ideal. "Angela and Caroline both come to school on the bus," she grinned, "they were witches as well ..."

"You'll make lots more friends as a day girl," her mother nodded. "In fact, I'm thinking of having a Christmas party so that I get to know some of the mothers!"

Neil looked up as his father came back into the room. "That was Jimmy MacFarlane," he said. "He's asked us round to the farm tomorrow afternoon to meet some people from one of those English crop circle societies. Remember the night we saw the wheat making all those fantastic patterns, Neil?"

"Will I ever forget," Neil shivered. "That was scary!"

"Well, apparently Jimmy took pictures of the

field the next day and sold them to the *Berwickshire News* to make a bit of money. They splashed them all over the front page, of course, and the upshot of it all is that Jimmy's been approached by some members of a crop circle club who wanted to investigate the field. They're going to go over it with metal detectors to test it for signs of magnetism or some such thing."

"Do you think they'll find anything?" Neil frowned. "I mean ..."

"I shouldn't think so," her father said reassuringly. "The witches are far too clever to leave any traces behind."

34. Earth magic

"Hi," Jimmy MacFarlane grinned cheerily as the car drew up at the side of the road.

"We aren't interrupting you, are we?" John MacLean asked, looking across the yard at two men standing near the farmhouse door.

"Not at all," Jimmy smiled. "Come along and meet Tony and Bill, the crop circle fanatics I was telling you about. They're really anxious to meet you."

Tony and Bill looked in their twenties and waved a hand as they approached.

"This is John MacLean," Jimmy said, effecting introductions, "and his two kids, Neil and Clara. Neil was here with his dad when one of the crop circles was being made. In fact, he was in the field when the movement started."

"Really," the two men looked impressed as the farmer nodded towards the gate that led onto the field.

"That's the Home Field there."

Neil ran up to the gate and jumped onto it as he'd done before so that he could see out over the field. He heard Clara draw in her breath sharply, for Jimmy MacFarlane hadn't harvested the wheat; he'd left the crop in the field. He could still make out the patterns although bits of it seemed to have fallen apart but that wasn't what really stopped him short — it was the witches! Earth Witches! The field was full of them! Some were swooping over the field on broomsticks but, when they saw Neil and Clara, they flew to the side of the field and perched on the fence posts like huge black crows. Waiting! Watching!

"I couldn't harvest the crop," Jimmy explained, leaning on the gate. "It was a complete loss so I thought I'd leave it and maybe make some money out of television and the papers. I haven't covered my losses yet," he added, "but I've managed to make quite a bit out of it! They pay well for good stories and crop circles are always news."

"Do you mind if we go into the field?" Tony asked.

"Help yourself," the farmer gestured invitingly as he pushed the gate open.

"Look at this, Bill," Tony muttered, bending down to heave at a swathe of stalks. "It must have taken some strength to flatten this bit here. I can barely lift it."

Neil and Clara wandered in after them and looked cautiously at the witches. Just what were they up to, perched here and there round the field, Neil wondered. Were they going to attack? He hadn't forgotten the strength of their power on the night they'd made the crop circle and shivered at the memory, remembering how the strange force had tried to pull him into the earth.

"Cripes," Tony muttered, "this is really something. And you say there was no one in the field?" he queried, turning to Neil. "What about UFOs? There weren't any of them around, were there?"

"UFOs? Oh, you mean flying saucer type things?" Neil grinned as he realized the track their minds were following. "No, not a sign of anything like that."

Jimmy MacFarlane, too, hid a smile. Flying saucers, he thought. What next?

"You see there must have been a considerable force at work to make all this," Bill pointed out, backing Tony up, "and it must have come from somewhere!" He gestured round the field. "If there was no human help ... well, it's reasonable to suppose that someone or something non-human, so to speak, made them."

"I felt there was some sort of force," Neil admitted. "Maybe it was because I'd been hiding in the field when it all started. I felt it pulling *me* down as well as the wheat. It was really scary."

"Maybe we should get out the metal detectors," Tony said suddenly, "and give the field the once over." He looked at the farmer enquiringly. "You don't mind, do you?" he asked. "We've got all our gear in the van."

"Go ahead," the farmer smiled. "It'd be great if you found something! Preferably buried treasure! These blasted crop circles have just about ruined me."

As Jimmy Macfarlane and their father wandered off towards the farmhouse, Neil and Clara perched on the gate and, like the witches, watched Tony and Bill quarter the field, moving the metal detectors from side to side as they moved steadily across. Suddenly, Tony gave a shout and waved at Neil. "Ask the farmer for a couple of spades," he yelled. "We've picked something up!"

Mr MacFarlane nodded his head when asked for spades and pointed to a shed where a variety of tools hung on the walls. Neil ran across and lifting down two spades, carried them over his shoulder into the field. The witches, he noticed, seemed to have sensed that something untoward was happening and were slipping from their perches on the wall.

"Good lad," Tony said, taking the spades and passing one to Bill, "there's definitely something here." Both men stripped off their jackets, handed them to Neil and started to dig. Once they'd cleared the remains of the crop, they made quick progress and as the trench deepened, so the piles of earth grew on either side.

Neil was almost hopping up and down with excitement and the witches, too, edged closer until they stood in an interested ring round the digging. Clara eyed them warily, glad that they didn't seem threatening.

The witches pressed closer as Bill brushed his hair from his eyes. "I've got a strange feeling that we're onto something here," he said.

Clara nodded. It was the presence of the witches. She, too, could feel it. The atmosphere was heavy, threatening and yet exciting, too. The witches weren't exactly dancing up and down to see what was in the trench that Tony and Bill were digging, but they were peering down with expectant looks on their faces.

Neil tensed as he watched them, suddenly realizing there *was* something buried down there. The witches knew it and were waiting for it to be discovered.

"Don't expect too much," Tony cautioned, looking up at Neil, "it'll probably turn out to be some old piece of farm equipment that was buried ages ago."

"I don't know," Bill contradicted him, "this has a different feel to it somehow ..."

Clara's eyes were sparkling with excitement. "Wouldn't it be *great* if you made a real find!" she said.

It was then that Tony's spade struck something hard. "Give me some room, Bill!" he said excitedly. "I've hit something!"

By this time, the trench they'd dug was quite deep and Neil gave Bill a hand as he clambered out. Tony put his spade to one side and started scrabbling about with his hands in the earth. They heard his gasp of triumph as he sat back in the trench with a bit of a thump.

"What is it?" Bill asked, bending down. "What've you found? Anything valuable?"

"I'll say," Tony stood up, his head popping above the top of the trench. "Tell me this isn't gold!" He held up a goblet encrusted with earth but where the dirt had rubbed off, it showed raised, decorated motifs and it glinted yellow.

"Wow," Neil and Clara looked at one another in excitement. "Gold!"

The witches hissed with excitement and flapped around Tony, trying to touch the goblet.

"Right! We stop here," Bill said authoritatively. "Out you get, Tony," and he gave him a hand to scramble out of the hole.

They had almost reached the edge of the field when his father and Jimmy MacFarlane wandered up to the gate, deep in conversation.

The farmer stopped in mid-sentence, however, as Tony held up the goblet. He'd used his jacket to brush the bulk of the dirt off it and it now glinted yellow in the pale, winter sun. Neil, Clara, Bill and the entire coven of witches stood behind him as he smiled broadly at the farmer.

"You're in luck, Mr MacFarlane," Tony said formally, "by the look of it, I'd say it was Roman and it's most certainly gold."

Jimmy MacFarlane's face was a picture. "You mean ... you mean, you've *found* treasure?" he whispered, stretching out his hand for the goblet as though in a dream.

"It's a huge hoard, Jimmy," Bill said as Tony handed it over. "The detectors were all over the place!"

"You won't have to worry about harvesting your crops now," Tony grinned. "With gold prices what they are nowadays, you'll probably end up a millionaire!"

After they'd finished oohing and aahing over the goblet, John Maclean decided it was time for them to leave. Tony and Bill wanted to use the phone to contact a friend who was an expert on Roman artefacts, and he didn't want to be in the way.

"All very exciting, Jimmy," John smiled, "but we won't stop. You look like having a full house without adding us to the mix!"

"I still can't quite believe it's happened," the farmer said seriously. "You know, at one time, what with all the crop circles and all, I really thought we were going to have to sell up."

"Yes," Clara said without thinking, "the witches did you a good turn after all."

Neil looked at her sharply and jabbed her in the ribs. There was a brief silence and she turned scarlet as she realized what she'd just said.

"Word's got around already, has it?" the farmer smiled. "I'm not surprised. The farm's been in the family for generations and it's a tradition that if we look like losing our land we go to Witches' Wood and threaten the witches."

"You threatened the witches?" John MacLean said in surprise.

"I know it sounds daft," Jimmy admitted, looking slightly shamefaced. "The men thought I'd gone off my rocker as well, but I was at the end of my tether and quite frankly, I'd had enough. Last week, I got them all together and we went out to Witches' Wood loaded up with chainsaws, mechanical diggers ... the lot!" He laughed suddenly. "We must have looked like basket cases," he admitted, "clustered round the wood looking like a demolition squad gone wrong, but I told the witches fair and square that if they didn't do something to save Blackriggs, I'd level Witches' Wood to the ground and I brought a couple of the diggers into the field to prove my point."

Neil and Clara exchanged knowing smiles, imagining the consternation that that must have caused. "I bet that put Maritza in a *real* flap," Neil whispered.

"Well, it certainly worked," their father looked at Jimmy MacFarlane with some amusement as they reached the car. "Now look what's happened! Buried treasure!" Jimmy MacFarlane nodded but his face was thoughtful as he turned slightly and looked over the expanse of neatly ploughed brown fields to the distant stand of black, leafless trees that rose eerily against a grey winter sky that was the colour of pewter.

"Aye, the threat worked right enough," Jimmy MacFarlane said, "but you know what it means, don't you?"

The MacLeans eyed one another sideways. The farmer's gaze was still fixed on the distant hill but he turned and, as he looked at them, answered his own question. "It means, doesn't it, that there really *are* witches in Witches' Wood!" he said slowly, "Which would be why my fields were full of pentagrams. It was the witches!"

"You could well be right," John MacLean admitted, glancing at Neil and Clara as the witches gathered to watch them leave.

Neil nodded in agreement. "I wouldn't worry about it, Mr MacFarlane," he said lightly. "If there *are* witches in Witches' Wood then this is *their* home, too, and from now on, I reckon they're *always* going to be on your side."

As he said this, both children looked beyond the farm gate to where Maritza stood, broomstick at the ready. Her cloak fluttered dramatically in the breeze and there was a hissing from the rest of the coven as they piled in behind her, their faces strong and fierce. Maritza scowled at Neil's words but the look in her eyes told both children that she'd got the message. She looked at them speculatively for a long moment but her gaze was not unfriendly as, with a wry smile, she bowed mockingly and, lifting her hand, gave the signal to leave.

The witches immediately slipped onto their broomsticks and Clara caught her breath at the sight of them rising into the air in a swirl of black robes like a cloud of monstrous crows. As the coven wheeled over the fields and swooped away towards Witches' Wood, however, the atmosphere lightened noticeably as a sudden shaft of pale winter sunshine pierced the leaden sky and made the air sparkle.

Jimmy MacFarlane, following their glances, looked at them strangely. If he guessed that they could see something that was hidden from him, he said nothing but, like them, he knew within himself that, after this, there would be no more trouble from the witches.